Hi Rosie

Hope u enjoy the book

Lov
Sinda

D1333129

THE MRS MARRIDGE PROJECT

THE MRS MARRIDGE PROJECT

Pauline Fisk

faber and faber

First published in 2005
by Faber and Faber Limited
3 Queen Square London WC1N 3AU

Typeset by Faber and Faber Ltd
Printed in England by Mackays of Chatham plc, Chatham, Kent

A CIP record for this book
is available from the British Library

ISBN 0–571–22687–6

2 4 6 8 10 9 7 5 3 1

To Nat and Virpi

Contents

Prologue: The Epiphany

Halfway through my sister's best friend's funeral, I decided to get married. I knew I wasn't old enough, but life felt too short to hang about. You took a breath and it was over, and you'd never done a thing you wanted. Lucy Chan never got a single benefit from her years of studying for university. She was dead, run over by a car, before she'd even sat an A-level exam.

The church was packed. Half our town was there, and half our school as well. Everyone was crying, especially my sister Kate. I should have been crying too, because I'd known Lucy my whole life. But grief can do funny things to you, as I was discovering. Instead of shedding tears, I couldn't help thinking that Lucy's life would have been better spent having fun. Filling it with school work felt like a terrible mistake – and it was just the sort of mistake that I would make!

Lucy was a slogger, just like me. She was one of those hard-working, determined types who always put their grades ahead of everything else. The type who sets her mind to things, and has the drive to make them happen.

'That Lucy Chan!' people used to say. 'She's a real go-getter. There's nothing she can't do, if she sets her mind to it. Once she gets the bit between her teeth, there's no stopping her.'

This was all very well, but being a go-getter hadn't saved Lucy's life when some drunk was in a hurry to get home and watch the rugby on the telly. And suddenly I worried that it wouldn't save my life either. I could run along the sea wall, like little Johnny Williams, and a freak wave could sweep me out to sea. Or wake up one morning, like our old dog Tramp, and find I had a terrible disease. One day, he'd been a happy little terrier, chewing sticks, and the next he'd been down at the vet's in the final stages of leukaemia. Nobody had known that anything was wrong until he went and died – and a thing like that could happen to anyone!

Lucy's coffin started up the aisle, followed by her family staring straight ahead, trying to be brave but looking desperate. It was the same all over the church. The coffin glided between us, a white island, sweet with the scent of lilies, in a sea of black, bowed heads. Mum wept as if Lucy had been a member of our own family. Life without her would never be the same. Even Dad wept, his knack of seeing the funny side of things at unlikely times and in unlikely places temporarily suspended.

And as for Kate – well, what can I say? Her shoulders heaved and tears poured down her face as if they'd never stop. Kate had never been the crying type, and I was seriously worried. I wanted to comfort her – to be there for her like a sister should – but suddenly a chasm seemed to lie between us. I couldn't reach her or grieve with her. To be honest, I couldn't even reach myself. The chasm lay across my life, cutting off my feelings from everything else. I was ashamed to be dry-eyed while everybody else wept. But there was nothing I could do about it. For some strange reason, instead of grieving for Lucy, the only person I could grieve for was – *me*.

'If *I* was in that coffin,' I thought, 'my whole life would have been wasted. Everything I'd ever done would have been for nothing. None of it would matter. I'd have died without knowing who I really was, or getting what I wanted out of life. I wouldn't even *know* what I wanted out of life. I mean, I wouldn't have a clue.'

Lucy's coffin reached the chancel steps and came to rest before the altar. Her family filed into the front pews and sat down. The congregation sat down too, but I remained standing, lost in a tangle of thoughts. Only yesterday, my headmistress, Ms Lloyd-Roberts, had said that the path to true happiness lay in finding the right career. But if I died before I found that career, did that mean I'd never known true happiness?

Mum poked me to sit down, and Kate hissed at me to 'stop acting weird'. I sank onto the pew, mortally ashamed of having spent a single moment thinking of anybody other than Lucy and her family. The priest climbed into the pulpit and started delivering his address. Kate wrung her hands. Mum buried her face in a box of tissues that she'd brought especially. The boy on the other side of her wept so much that Mum leant across and shared her tissues with him.

He was a gorgeous boy, black-haired and slim, with an elegance about him that not even swollen eyes and a dripping nose could disguise. I didn't know who he was but found myself fantasizing that he'd been Lucy's secret lover. At least, I hoped he had. I hoped she'd had a life before she died.

The priest started on about heaven, and I imagined Lucy stuck up there for ever, a legendary virgin like Ida Jones from Back Street, whose greatest claim to fame, at her old age, was that she'd never been kissed. Not that I knew, of course, that Lucy'd been a virgin. If she'd gone out with that boy, she must at least have done a bit of fooling around.

But if she hadn't, did it really matter? Would she be a lesser person for it? Was that all there was to life – a bit of fooling around, a few exams with straight A grades, the promise of university at the end of it all and a career if you were lucky?

Or was there more?

The priest finished his address and we started singing what the family said was Lucy's 'favourite hymn'. I looked at her coffin covered in white lilies. Sunlight danced on it, falling from a stained-glass window depicting the Holy Family. The colours in the window were a stunning contrast to the black-garbed congregation in the pews, and the serene faces of the Holy Family a stunning contrast to the tears around me. An angel looked down upon them, wearing an expression of serenity too. There were no tears for them. No fears of what the future might bring. No death hanging over them, full of cruel surprises.

They were frozen in a moment of perfect peace, and I envied them. I really did. My life had been thrown into turmoil by the events of the last couple of weeks. Until then, I'd never really grasped the fact that people like me died. It was always other people who did things like that. People somewhere else – old people, stupid kids who did things for a dare or people on the telly. Definitely not people whose lives touched mine.

I had thought I was immortal, and the world around me charmed, but not any more. Everything had changed for ever. I didn't know what the future would bring, or even if imagining I'd have a future was expecting too much. Didn't know where I was going in life. Didn't know what I wanted to get out of it. I felt as if I was standing on a precipice with nothing to hold on to. It was a terrifying prospect.

We finished the hymn and Lucy's father went to the lectern to read a eulogy. He got halfway through but couldn't carry on. For a moment it was as if he too was standing on a precipice, but then Lucy's mother went and stood beside him and read the words where he'd left off. They stood together, shoulder to shoulder and hand in hand. They were both crying, but they got through together, turn and turn about.

I watched them doing it, helping each other through, and suddenly – like that eureka moment in the bath, if you know the story of Archimedes – I *did* know what I wanted after all. It was very simple. *I wanted to be like them.* They were safe because, whatever came along, they had each other. They were strong because they stuck together. You could feel them reaching out, their voices answering each other as if they were one. For richer, for poorer, in sickness and in health, they were there for each other, and that closeness of theirs – that sense of belonging – was what I wanted for myself.

'It's people who make all the difference,' I thought, 'not school work and exams. My path to true happiness doesn't lie in straight "A" grades. If I could only have what they've got, then I could face anything. What I really want in life is to fall in love and marry. *To find my Mr Right and become his wife!*'

I must have gasped, because people turned and looked at me. But who could blame me if I did? Marriage wasn't exactly a subject I'd ever given much thought to. Nobody in our family had ever gone in for it, apart from Grandad – and he wasn't exactly a role model! According to Mum, it was only brainless film stars who got married these days, because they were the only ones who could afford the maintenance. It certainly wasn't something to be considered before a woman hit her thirties, and even then it was a pretty risky idea.

'But why?' I asked myself. 'I don't get it. What's wrong with marriage?'

What indeed! Suddenly it wasn't good enough to have a string of lovers, every one as gorgeous as the boy next to Mum. Before I went and died like Lucy, I wanted somebody to fall in love with me, and fill me with serenity, like the Holy Mother in the stained-glass window. I wanted them to be there for me, always seeing the best in me. And, most of all, I wanted them to commit their lives to me, loving me enough to marry me.

Mum might call that sort of thing a fairy tale, but

why couldn't fairy tales ever come true? I imagined the church full of pink fluffy roses instead of waxy, death-mask lilies, and everybody smiling instead of weeping, and me, glamorous in tight white silk, chucking my bouquet for one of my girlfriends to catch – preferably Jenna, but I wouldn't mind if it was Jody or Rebecca.

In school, weeks later, my English teacher, Mrs Arrol, explained about epiphanies. These were moments when your life was changed for ever because you got some sort of revelation. As literary devices went, epiphanies were dangerously over-used, according to Mrs Arrol. But, over-used or not, that moment in church was mine.

There wasn't anything else that it could be. I sat there in astonishment, struggling with the fact that marriage could be the 'career for me'. The career that Ms Lloyd-Roberts had said I had a duty to work towards with single-minded dedication for the rest of my school life.

By the time the eulogy was over I could scarcely stop myself from smiling. Mum and Dad would go up the wall if they knew what I was thinking, but I didn't care. They'd had my life mapped out almost since I was born, enrolling me into an all-girls school in the hope that nothing – i.e. boys – would distract me from the higher calling of academic success. It had cost them a fortune to send me to Fishguard Girls' Academy, but I didn't care about that either. Not when the perfect man was out there somewhere, waiting to fall in love with me and marry me and make me happy for how-ever many years I'd got left.

I sang the final hymn with a lustiness that was almost obscene. Dad glanced at me as if afraid that grief was tipping me over the brink. Mum hissed at me to sing more quietly. Kate scowled because Lucy had been her friend, not mine, and if anybody deserved people's glances it definitely wasn't me.

Finally the service drew to a close. The priest prayed for Lucy's soul and I prayed for my own, asking God to keep me going until the legal age of marriageability. It was all very well having some future husband out there waiting for me, but some future drink-driver could be out there too. Either that or some unknown medical condition, waiting to take hold of my body – Sudden Adult Death Syndrome, which I'd heard about on the telly, or something like leukaemia that humans got as well as dogs.

The coffin started on its final journey down the aisle and everybody stood. Slowly, it passed out of church and out of our lives. By the time we'd followed it out-side, the immediate family party had moved on to the crematorium. We stood blinking in the golden light of an autumn morning. The whole thing was over, just like Lucy's life. I wanted to tell Kate how sorry I was that she'd lost her friend but, for once, I didn't know where to start.

Neither of us said a word as we walked together to the village hall, where a lunch of savoury snacks had been provided by the Chan family. We didn't feel like eating, but queued up like everybody else to put something on our plates. Then we walked to the end of the hall to look at a memorial display of photographs that had been set up on a low dais, with a black sash hanging over them.

Most of the photos portrayed Lucy as a baby, a toddler or a serious little girl with jet-black hair, rarely smiling and always looking deadly earnest. My three favourites, however, were of her with their family dog, laughing as they played together; with her friends, including Kate, sunbathing on the beach; and with her GCSE certificates, standing to attention in school uniform, her proud smile like sunlight on a cloudy day.

I had to walk away. Suddenly I found myself crying. *At last* I was crying! The relief was overwhelming, but Kate was furious with me for making an exhibition of myself. If I had to cry, she said, I should have done it in church like everybody else, not here in the village hall over a plateful of savoury snacks.

'Pull yourself together,' she hissed. 'Everybody's staring.'

This only served to make things worse. I cried and

couldn't stop, and Mum said I should have known the funeral would be too much for me and never have come. 'Think of other people's feelings,' she said. 'Especially your poor sister's. Either get a grip or return to school.'

This was rich, coming from Mrs Kleenex herself! It was also a wonderful example of the cunning way Mum's mind works, never letting an opportunity pass her by. Half my teachers were in that village hall, and a good number of fellow pupils and their parents, but I couldn't see anyone else being cajoled into returning to school.

'Just because you blew your own education,' I hissed, 'that doesn't give you the right to interfere with mine!'

Mum didn't like that one bit. She pursed her lips together and said, 'Maybe you're right. Maybe I *did* blow my education. Maybe I had the brains but didn't use them, and ended up in some crummy job that bored me rigid. But I'll be damned if I'm going to let the same thing happen to you!'

I didn't answer. It wasn't worth the bother. This was a well-worn argument, used against both Kate and me any time Mum thought that we were slacking. The best thing to do was walk away from it. So that's what I did. I shut Mum up by doing what she wanted and going back to school.

Here my new-found ambition to get married took something of a knocking. It was English after lunch, and maybe men were glorious in books like *Pride and Prejudice* but, in Physics afterwards, my teacher, Mr Pugh, was a total pain. He always looked so nice and kind and friendly, and that's probably what Mrs Pugh thought when she married him, but he spent his every spare minute making our lives a misery – either that or chasing women, and the whole school knew it, and probably half of Fishguard too.

Being married didn't stop him. It didn't stop my friend Rebecca's father either, who was just the same. And maybe my friend Jody's stepfather didn't chase women, but nobody would ever want him, apart from his wife. I mean, who'd fall for a small-town vet who looked and smelt like a ferret, and spent his whole life up to his elbows in animals' backsides?

By the time I got home, I'd convinced myself that the funeral had worked me up into some weird mental state and marriage wasn't what I wanted after all. It was only for women whose careers were floundering, or who were panicking about being too old to have babies. It had nothing to do with love and serenity – and absolutely nothing to do with being fourteen.

Next day, however, buying chips after school, I caught sight of that boy again – the one I'd thought was Lucy's lover. He'd exchanged his smart black suit for an apron with 'Charlie's Takeaway' written on it, and was serving behind the till. But he still looked terrific, and I broke out in a sweat and had to turn and walk away. Anybody else would have simply fancied him and been done with it, but I had to find my mind full of marriage again.

It was ridiculous, but I couldn't help myself. I knew that boy couldn't possibly be my Mr Right because he was too gorgeous to ever fancy me, and I was too young for him anyway. I mean, he had to be a good three years older than me.

But if I couldn't marry him, then someone else had to be out there waiting instead. For suddenly – without a shadow of doubt – I knew that marriage was my destiny. There was no point telling myself that this could only be a fairy tale, or that the funeral had messed me up inside my head.

Some girls dreamt of being pop stars when they grew up, or scientists, or astronauts, or hairdressers, or nuns. They couldn't explain why – it was just what they wanted. They had their vocations, and I mightn't be able to explain either but, from that moment onwards, outside Charlie's Takeaway, *I knew that this was mine.*

Cookery

*
*
*
*
*

Part I
Research

APPLICATION
IS THE
KEY

Division of labour
Property prices
DIY

Weddings

* * * * * * * * * * * *

Babies
Sex
Men

1
Finding the Key

The key to passing exams is application. I know this for a fact because Ms Lloyd-Roberts told us so in assembly the day after the funeral. We were embarking on the GCSE syllabus, she said, and we must be wondering what we were in for. But we weren't to worry because, however hard things got, we were bound to succeed if we only applied ourselves.

'And by succeed,' she said, 'I don't just mean top grades, but achieving all your other goals as well. Passing exams is a vital step in scaling slopes as high as any Everest. But in your lifetime of achievement, it's only the first step. Don't you ever forget that.'

I mightn't forget, but I didn't necessarily understand. I shuffled restlessly, and so did everybody else. When Ms Lloyd-Roberts started on like that, we knew there'd be no stopping her. Sure enough, she carried on, blithely unaware of the confusion she was causing, talking about good foundations and building on our skills, essay by essay and brick by brick. Her Everest example was only the start of it. Comparisons were made between coursework and plumbing, electrical circuitry and exam success. And the purpose of it all, we were assured, was that the House of Knowledge would be our very own.

'If my dad knew I was being trained for the building trade, he'd want his school fees back,' Rebecca Edwards whispered, rolling her eyes.

'You think you've got something to moan about?' I said. 'I've heard it all before. This is just the way my mother talks. It drives me crazy.'

Finally we filed out of the school hall, Ms Lloyd-Roberts's final words ringing in our ears that we should, 'Go forth and multiply your knowledge and enjoyment of the world. And don't forget, girls – *application's the key*.' She beamed down at us, confident in the belief that she'd demystified the GCSE process and passed on something of vital importance for the next two years, if not the rest of our lives.

As soon as I left the hall, however, I put the whole thing out of my mind. I had other matters to think about – more important ones as well, like getting married. When I want something, I always have a strategy; short- and long-term objectives, plans and endless lists. I'm not the sort of person who can ever let a thing 'just happen'.

But how to start on something like this? It was

hardly the sort of project that I could discuss with my form tutor and, if I told my friends, they'd think that I was mad. As for my family — I'd never hear the end of it. As far as Dad was concerned, marriage was a ball and chain, only there for losers who put their trust in bits of paper. Mum said the divorce rate spoke for itself. And her sister, Jane, who lives up the other end of Goat Street from us, said that there wasn't a man alive who any woman could sensibly spend a lifetime with.

Even Jane's on-off boyfriend, Carl, felt the same, saying that the only way he'd ever tie the knot was if they let you marry more than one wife at a time.

Well, *that* wasn't the sort of marriage I had in mind! It was the boy-meets-girl, loves-girl-and-she-loves-him type of marriage, celebrated with a great big wedding and a happily ever after ending. The sort of marriage that you read about in novels, or see in films starring people like Julia Roberts and Hugh Grant.

But how could I tell anyone that this was what I wanted for myself? And, more to the point, how could I find someone to marry me before cruel fate took over and I went and died? By night, I'd lie awake asking myself this question, and by day, I'd scour the newspapers, looking for advice. I'd had obsessions before, like my astronaut phase, when I'd written to NASA and the European Space Programme, asking if they'd take me for work experience, and my actress phase, when I sent a letter to Catherine Zeta Jones's mam, who lived up the road from my great-aunt Blanche, asking for help. But this was different. I'd never felt so passionate about anything as I now did about getting married.

I cut out articles on film stars' marriages, royal marriages – including morganatic marriages – gay marriages, so-called immigration marriages, arranged marriages, serial marriages and teenage marriages, trying to understand what my obsession was all about. I read news items on fathers' rights, gypsy marriages and child slave brides, trawled through the letters pages in my sister's magazines and my parents' weekend newspapers, and drooled over photographs in *Vogue* of brides in state-of-the-art wedding frocks. But, despite my mounting box of cuttings, I still felt none the wiser.

What made the state of marriage so different to flat-sharing, for example, or joining a commune or living together like Mum and Dad? And as for getting married itself – how was I meant to make it happen? I didn't have a clue.

But then, one night my headmistress's words came back to me. I was lying in bed, staring blankly at the ceiling as usual, and suddenly it occurred to me that if application was the key to passing my exams, it could also be the key to getting married. The two weren't all that different. Both were gateways into adult life. Both required careful planning. Both had the power to change lives. And both – I suddenly realized – could be achieved in exactly the same way.

'Of course,' I thought. 'It's obvious! Maybe I don't have all the answers, but *I know where to start!*'

I leapt out of bed and started rummaging through my schoolbooks, looking for my GCSE timetable for the next two years. I had class tests after Christmas, end-of-year exams next summer, mocks the following winter, study leave the following spring and what my teachers called 'the real thing' after that – a string of GCSE exams that would take place in May and June the summer after next.

Within that outer framework, however, there was another tighter structure – an intricate pattern of research, case studies, field trips, coursework and revision, giving shape and substance to every minute of the next two years. But could it also give shape to my new ambition?

I knew it could. 'If I get this right,' I thought, 'I can actually be married the summer after next! It might sound crazy, but I know that I can pull it off. Mum and Dad will hate it, but I've got two years to work on that one. All I have to do is *apply myself!*'

I wrote the words 'APPLICATION IS THE KEY' in my diary. Then, as if I thought I might forget them, I tore out the page and stuck it over my desk. My mobile started bleeping, Jenna texting me to say goodnight, but I didn't text back as usual. I was too busy listing all the stages I'd have to go through in order to succeed in becoming a grade-A wife. My hands were shaking as I wrote everything down. It was as if I'd cracked a code and could read my future like a secret message. I wrote 'Research', 'Case Studies', 'Field Trip', 'Coursework', 'Revision', 'Mocks', 'Study Leave' and 'The Real Thing'.

By the time I'd finished, Jenna was on the phone, wanting to know why I hadn't replied. We chattered about nothing in particular until she fell asleep. But I lay wide awake, wishing I could sleep too but nursing a thumping headache. It was hardly surprising after so much excitement, but I made a note of it in the back of my diary, where I kept a detailed record of my personal health.

'Nothing to worry about, I'm sure,' I wrote, but put an asterisk in the margin so that it would show if a pattern was emerging.

At long last I fell asleep, but no sooner had I closed my eyes, or so it seemed to me, than it was morning. The sun came pouring through the curtains, shining on my desk and the message hanging over it. Application was every bit as much the key in the bright light of day as it had been last night, and I leapt out of bed and dashed to my desk, where I started drawing up a list of research subjects.

'Babies' went onto that list, along with 'love', 'sex', 'weddings', 'men', 'religion', 'cookery', 'divisions of labour', 'property prices' and 'DIY'. I could have carried on as well – so totally absorbed that I forgot to wash and dress and was nearly late for school.

Finally, however, realizing how late I was, I hid the list in a desk drawer and rushed off without breakfast. Usually I met Jenna outside, and Jody and Rebecca down at the crossroads, but all three of them had gone by the time I appeared – and so had the school bus.

Not that I cared. It was nice to be alone and to have time to think. I sat in the bus shelter, waiting for the scheduled service to come along, watching sleepy little Newport coming to life. Our town's not like Fish-guard, which is full of cars and shoppers, and has a business park, supermarkets, a railway station and a ferry terminal to Ireland. There are just a few rows of fishermen's cottages, a handful of shops, a couple of pubs, the rugby club and the primary school. Oh, and the yacht club, of course.

In the summer the holidaymakers come down with their cars and yachts and windsurf boards, and every house in town is full. But in the winter Newport's really quiet, apart from first thing in the morning, when people go to work or school, and teatime, when they come home again.

I watched mums with pushchairs making their way

down the street, and cars jostling for position as they got caught up in the traffic at the bottom of the road between the school gate and the estuary. Jody's mum went by with a carload of toddlers for the nursery school, and came back with it empty. She offered me a lift into Fishguard, and I thanked her and got in. I wouldn't have minded staying at the bus stop all day, thinking my thoughts and watching the world passing by, but I knew it would only get me into trouble.

Jody's mum talked all the way to Fishguard, but I didn't hear a word. Normally I'm pretty chatty myself, so perhaps that's why, when she dropped me off, she said, 'Are you all right, Elin? You don't seem to be yourself today.'

'I'm fine,' I said. 'Really. Thanks for the ride.'

Jody's mum wasn't the only person who asked if I was all right that day. So many people asked that I ended up with a headache from repeating, 'Honestly, I'm fine.' It was a relief to get home, close the door on the lot of them, and get on with the only thing that really mattered in my life – *marriage plans*.

I opened up my diary, drew a line under everything I'd written so far, recorded the exact time, as if it was a significant moment in world history, and wrote END OF OLD LIFE, START OF NEW. Then I took the research list I'd hidden in my drawer and started work in earnest.

On a fresh page, I wrote my aim – to be married on my sixteenth birthday, 31 August, in two years' time, which was the first day when I'd be old enough, in law, to become a wife. Then I started brainstorming. I went down that list, scribbling every thought-association that came into my head, and became so carried away with it all that I started recording ridiculous things, like what hair colour I preferred in my ideal husband, and the names I'd give our children.

Welsh names were out. Names like Jez and Baz and Zak were in. And my husband would be called Sebastian, or Seb for short, or Oliver or James. His eyes would be brown, and they'd be kind eyes and utterly trustworthy, but there'd be a hint of wickedness in them as well – something exciting that would set him apart.

I didn't mind how old he was, but he had to be smart. He had to be crazy about me too, head over heels in love. It would help if he had money – enough to get me a big, flashy diamond ring, not to say anything of a wedding dress out of *Vogue* – and I wouldn't exactly object if he drove around in something really cool, like a Porsche. That would definitely be one up on Mum and Dad, who drove a clapped-out Mazda known universally as the 'Millennium Falcon', and Rebecca's family with their boring BMWs.

Page after page, I wrote this down until I finally

realized what a load of rubbish it was, and tore it up and threw it in the bin. Apart from the bit about love, there was scarcely a word on any of those pages that had anything to do with the real me, or what I wanted out of life, or how I intended to make my marriage work when I'd found my Mr Right.

It was as if I was running away from the real project ahead of me, sensing how difficult and challenging it was going to be. For the first time, it dawned on me exactly what I'd taken on. Marriage was a tricky business – not just the getting married either, but staying that way. You only had to read the newspapers to see that. I thought of all those rich and famous people whose marriages had failed. It made you think. It really did. The wonder was that people still wanted to go through with it.

And yet they did. Year by year, all around the planet, in every race and culture, people still got married.

'It speaks for itself,' I thought. 'There has to be a way of making a success of it, otherwise people wouldn't bother.'

But figuring out what that way might be, and then getting it down on paper, were proving far more difficult than I'd expected. I sat for ages, writing things like 'It's important to communicate,' and, 'You need a bit of give and take.' But I knew I was only scraping the surface. There was so much more to it all than that.

And, besides, I wasn't answering the question of how to find a husband in the first place.

When Mum called me down for supper, it came as a relief. It was a special family supper too. Grandad had come round, and Dad was home early from work. Even Kate came down and ate with us instead of eating in her bedroom, over her homework.

The cause of our celebration was Jane, who'd just come out of hospital with her brand-new baby daughter, Imogen Louise. She was a beautiful-looking baby with flawless skin and ginger hair, but she cried most of the time, not even stopping when we drank her health in sparkling wine. Not that Jane seemed to mind. After seven long days in hospital, fighting doctors, nurses and midwives, she was happy to be back again in the bosom of the family.

We're a funny lot, our family – as thick as thieves, but continually fighting. But then, an old grump like Grandad – Dad's words, not mine – couldn't possibly have had daughters who didn't enjoy an argument from time to time. Even Kate can be an old grump, and Dad's not much better sometimes.

All the way through supper, they argued about everything that you could think of. Even Imogen Louise couldn't shut them up. God, politics, the pros and cons of breast-feeding – they argued about it all. I sat back and watched. There was Kate, who'd been so quiet since Lucy's funeral, getting animated and chipping in; Dad big and brawny, rolling up his sleeves as the argument got heavy; Mum small and tight in a sweater that had shrunk because she'd washed it on the wrong setting, insisting that only she was right; Jane trying to have the last word over the din of Imogen Louise; and Grandad, who couldn't hear most of the argument but reckoned he didn't need to anyway, because he knew better than anybody else.

What bound us all together, I wondered? Was it simply blood relationships, or was there more to it than that? We thought we knew each other through and through, but did we really? Did *I* know them? Did *they* know me? Was I just that little girl, to them, who appeared in all the family photographs, her hair tied up in bunches and braces on her teeth? Or had they noticed I'd grown up, and was old enough to plan a marriage?

As soon as the meal was over I tore back upstairs, saying I had mountains of work to do. Somehow I had to turn my messy brainstorming into a proper structure with dates on it so that, when the Big Day came, I'd be as ready for it as any GCSE.

Before I could do that, however – in fact, before I could do anything else – I had some important questions to ask. I'd been thinking about them all through supper, and now I got out my diary and started writing them down. After 'Research' and somewhere between 'Case Studies', 'Field Trip' and 'Revision', I promised myself I'd produce an essay on each question and store it under the heading 'Coursework'.

'*What is Marriage?*' I wrote, followed by '*How to Recognize Mr Right*', '*How to Keep Him When You've Found Him*', '*What's Wrong with Marrying at Sixteen?*', '*The Pros and Cons of Babies*', '*How to Stop Them Screaming*' and '*What is Love?*'

Once I'd started, there was no stopping me. I lay awake for hours that night, thinking in the darkness. '*Why Get Married?*' I thought, and '*What's It Going to be Like?*', and I was still coming up with questions in the morning. In fact, I was so busy getting them down that I was late again for the school bus.

This time it was Dad who, finding me sitting in the shelter, drove me to Fishguard. He was late for work himself, but scolded me all the way to school for what he called my bad time-keeping. This was totally unjust, but later that very same day I had reason to dwell upon the fact that men *were* sometimes unjust, and there was nothing you could do to change them.

It was Mr Pugh, our Physics teacher, who got me thinking that way, shouting at us for not finishing a piece of Physics homework that he hadn't even given us. We tried to point this out to him, but he shouted even more and refused to listen to a word we said.

Afterwards, everybody grumbled about him. 'Men are stupid,' Jody said, and Rebecca quoted her mother saying that all there was to know about them started and ended between their legs.

Everybody thought this was hysterical, except for me, who laughed along with all the rest but didn't quite get the joke. When I got home, I promised myself, I'd start my research on the thorny subject of 'Men'. Obviously I'd got a lot to learn.

To this end, I made another of my lists – a short but tricky affair listing the general areas I might want to investigate, though not knowing quite where to start. I cursed the fact that I didn't have a brother and that most of my school life had been spent with girls. There was no one I could ask to help me. Jenna had a brother, but he was away at university, and Jane's boyfriend, Carl, was out of favour at the minute, and the only other boys I knew were the ones who hung around outside school at the end of the day – and they'd never as much as looked my way.

But then that evening – as if designed especially to get my research going – Mum and Dad had an argument. I didn't know what had set it off because I was in my room at the time, but when I got downstairs it had blown out of all proportion. Mum was accusing Dad of doing nothing with his life except slumming in front of the telly watching kung-fu DVDs and boring reality TV shows about people like us having arguments about watching the telly. He refused to switch it off and she tried to make him by snatching the remote. They ended up screaming at each other. Mum accused Dad of being fat and he called her a nag.

'*A nag?*' she yelled, turning bright red. 'You think I *nag*? You think that *I* – who spend my whole life biting my tongue – nag *you*?! Why, if you ever listened, it'd be a different story. You try the patience of a saint, you really do. Any other woman would have dumped you years ago. I mean, look at you! Whatever happened to your get-up-and-go? You're like a lump of soggy bread. You're like a bowl of porridge. You're like . . .'

She ran out of words. Dad laughed as if he'd won, but in the end she succeeded in getting him off the sofa.

'Typical woman!' he grumbled as he stomped out of the room. 'You never know when to leave a chap alone. Thank God I never made the mistake of marrying you!'

'Typical man,' Mum shouted back, 'to think I'd ever *want* to!'

2

My Dad as a Man

After that, I started worrying about why my parents hadn't married. It had never been an issue before, but now I wanted to know. Was it really because they didn't believe in marriage, or had they simply never asked each other? Or was it that they didn't love each other as much as other people's parents? Had they only stayed together because of Kate and me? Or was Dad secretly married to someone else and had another family somewhere?

I knew it wasn't very likely, but I couldn't help thinking about it. I even sounded out Kate, to see what she thought. She laughed for just about the first time since Lucy's funeral, and said that I was being stupid.

'Of course there isn't any other family,' she said. 'Or a secret marriage either. Mum and Dad love each other. They're a pair of geek-heads who'd never as much as *look* at anybody else.'

Her words had the ring of truth about them and I started calming down. But I couldn't help wondering what life would have been like if Mum and Dad *had* married. Would Dad be an even worse telly addict than he was now? Would he still have put on weight, or be a worse couch potato? And what about Mum? Would she still nag? And why *did* she nag? Was it because men were impossible? Were women impossible as well, and if so why couldn't I see it?

I decided that if I was going to research 'Men', I might as well start with Dad. He was an obvious choice and, besides, who else had I got? I dug out my diary, wrote the words 'My Dad as a Man' and began on a positive note by listing all his finest qualities. There was the way he was always on my side when I fell out with my friends. And his smile, of course, which was the best in the world. And his sloppy jumpers, which I loved. And the way he played with Lizzie, our new terrier pup, teaching her tricks and being endlessly patient when she didn't get them.

He was really kind, my dad. I wrote that down as well. His life was a series of quiet good deeds, performed without fuss. He mightn't *want* to mend the neighbours' lawnmowers, do their shopping when their cars broke down or record their favourite programmes when they didn't have the time. But he was the one that people asked, and he always said yes.

'He always makes a joke of things as well,' I wrote. 'Poor old Dad – he has a terrible sense of humour.

And, on the subject of his other less than admirable qualities, his snore is legendary. So are the hours he spends in the loo, reading *Guardian* supplements, a week's worth at a time. And he's always having rows with Mum about ironing his shirts, as if he thinks he shouldn't have to do them. He's not exactly a *new man,* which is a shame for Mum, who probably didn't know that when she met him. They're always arguing about who does what on the domestic front. Sometimes Mum gets on her high horse, and sometimes Dad gets on his, and she usually wins, but he's usually the one who has the last word.'

My dad had got a way with words. I decided to put that at the top of both his lists – faults and good points. 'He's excellent at arguing,' I put. 'He has a real way of expressing himself. He can cut you down with just a word or two, but he can also really build you up.' Then I listed my favourite quotes.

'It's not what you dream about, it's what you do that counts.'

'Time doesn't stop for you when you cross the road.'

'Life's a barrel of beer, there for the drinking.'

'You've got to laugh or else you'll die.'

In no time at all, I had filled all the pages in my diary, including the spare ones for addresses, timetables and useful information. It was amazing how much I was digging up. I bought some new stationery in school — a stack of cardboard files, and books of A4 paper, a couple of scrapbooks, some homework rough work books and a big box folder to keep them all together.

Then I took them home, stashed the A4 paper in my desk drawer, and hid the rest in the big box folder, which I camouflaged with a label that read:

Year 10 English work on
'Love and Loss' –
The Mrs Marridge Project
by Samuel Beckett –
A Play for Our Times

I was confident that my parents, who never went to the theatre, wouldn't have a clue what Samuel Beckett had written — if they'd even heard of him!

All my newspaper cuttings about marriage went into the box, along with my old diary and my notes so far. It was the quickest-filling folder on my desk. If my class work folders had filled that quickly, my teachers would have been ecstatic. But I was too busy researching Dad to even think about school work, let alone do very much.

The more research I did, however, the more I found to do. I couldn't believe how much there was to be discovered on the subject of my dad. I listed all his interests, including the programmes that he watched on the telly and his inexplicable love of that whining Bob Dylan. I tried to work out what he liked about them all and if his interests formed a pattern. I listed his favourite writers alphabetically, from Martin Amis to Zane Grey. I listed his main topics of conversation, ranging from the downfalls of prime ministers, to how my school work was coming on, then back to politics again and what, according to his weekend *Guardian*, was happening on the world stage.

Then I studied all Dad's daily habits, embarking with the help of Microsoft Excel on a time-and-motion study that charted the way he spent his every minute. Day after day, I followed him around the house like a detective, timing everything he did with the second hand on my watch. I timed the processes he went through just to make a simple cup of tea, how long he spent in the bathroom, how long it took him to get out of the house in the morning, and even how long it took him to get to sleep at night – a mysterious procedure that required open windows and secret cigarettes.

I came up with results that Mum would have found fascinating if she'd ever got her hands on them. And that was just his home life. Heaven only knows what he was like at work.

Finally, I went through Dad's wardrobe, listing all his clothes down to the last pairless sock. I recorded what he ate, how much alcohol he drank and all the pills he took to give him extra boosts of Vitamin C and lower his cholesterol level.

Then I told myself my task was done. I'd got Dad pinned down from every angle. But did I understand him any better – and did I understand men, and what made them tick?

In a panic, I rewrote everything to make it clearer, putting it all into new sections with cross-references and better headings. But the more I tinkered, the more I felt removed from the ultimate objective of getting married. The mystery of how I was to find a man of my own was slipping further and further out of reach.

So – for that matter – was the mystery of why my parents had never married. One afternoon, home before everybody else, I went through all their old photographs. Dad had always been the one who kept them, rather than Mum. The recent ones were stored in a yellow plastic sack that grew larger and more tattered by the year, waiting for that illusive 'spare minute' when he'd put them into albums.

But a few of the old photographs – taken before Kate and I were born – were kept in a big box in the

23

back of the wardrobe, along with Mum's old red dress and Dad's terrible teenage poems. I sat with its contents spread out around me, feeling slightly guilty and hoping nobody would come in.

The photographs in front of me belonged to parents I didn't know, revealing a secret world that was all their own. One showed Mum with her hair right down her back, wearing the dress. Another showed her in denim dungarees, her hair cut shorter than a man's, and another showed her on a beach with hardly any clothes at all.

Then there were photographs of Dad, revealing tight trousers and a hitherto unknown interest in fashion. His hair was long, his eyes were dark and wild, he carried a guitar and he looked shockingly handsome for my dad.

He also looked shockingly young. They both did. It was weird to imagine them ever being like that. I found a photo of them snogging. Mum's arms were round Dad's neck, and his around her tiny waist, and I put the photo straight back and closed the box. The thought that my parents might once have had passionate, unbridled sex made me feel quite sick. I was glad Dad wasn't young any more. He might look handsome in the photographs but I preferred him now. Not for me some slim, lean dad who got chased by the girls, like Mick Jagger and Rebecca Edwards's father. I was happy with the dad I'd got – old and shambling and definitely undesirable to anyone but Mum.

That evening, I asked her what she'd thought of Dad the first time she'd set eyes on him. She made a joke about being drunk and not remembering. But, when I pressed her, she said that, actually, she'd been bowled over by his cleverness.

'You wouldn't believe the stuff he knew,' she said. 'He was a mine of information. I remember us camping on a beach somewhere. A whole crowd of us were there – I think it was just after we'd met. He knew every star in the sky – all the constellations and everything – and the name of every fossil. The beach was full of fossils too – I never saw so many in my life. And he knew the names of all the plants growing on the cliffs as well, and which ones were poisonous and which you could eat. I was dead impressed.' She smiled at the memory.

'Is that why you fell in love with him?' I said. 'Because he was good at naming things?'

Mum laughed. She was baking at the time, stretching and pounding a bowlful of dough and covering herself in flour. She didn't usually have time for what she called 'proper cooking', but when she did she always got in a mess.

'Who knows why anybody falls in love,' she said. 'It's not exactly something you can pin down. You'll find that out for yourself, one day. God – you've got it all to come! Though not yet, of course. That sort of thing is years away. For now you've got to concentrate on your GCSEs.'

There she was, doing it again – turning the conversation back to her advantage. 'But you and Dad,' I said, determined not to let her get away with it, 'what made you end up with each other rather than anybody else?'

'He may have ended up with me, but who says I've ended up with him?' Mum said, a steely twinkle in her eyes. 'Maybe I'm still waiting for my Mr Right.'

Later, I asked Dad about Mum. We were out with Lizzie on a training walk. She wasn't half as cute as Tramp, but was busy working her way into our hearts. We walked her along the sands on the far side of the estuary, then crossed the road bridge and followed the estuary along the town side, heading towards the yacht club and then back home.

It was a clear October day, almost as warm as summer – one of those days when you never want to stop. We walked along the seafront with its tall Victorian houses and sat at the end, outside Grandad's little beach hut. Here I worked the conversation round to Mum and casually slipped in a question about why she and Dad hadn't married. I tried to make it sound like no big deal but, all the same, Dad looked surprised.

'Did *she* get you to ask that,' he said, 'or are you ask-ing on your own account?'

'I'm asking because I want to know,' I said.

'Well, in that case,' Dad said, 'I suppose I didn't marry your mother because she wouldn't have wanted me to. She's a very independent woman, in case you hadn't noticed. And she's far too good for the likes of me. I mean, what would she ever see in me? And, besides, I never got round to asking. Life's so busy. You know what it's like.'

I did know what it was like. But, more than that, I knew what Dad was like. After tea that night, I wrote his answer up under four headings:

1) He refuses to take responsibility for his actions
2) He blames other people
3) He tries flattery to get out of things
4) He lets things slide.

After this, every time Dad said, 'I don't know, what do you think?' I filed it mentally under 1). Every time he said, 'You're the one who tidied things away,' I filed it under 2). Every time he said, 'I couldn't possibly do that – you're so much better than me,' I filed it under 3). And every time he said, 'Ask me tomorrow,' I filed it under 4).

3

The Grandad Crisis

After that, I didn't write much for a while. This was partly due to the fact that I was getting seriously behind on my school work, and partly due to something that Dad called 'The Grandad Crisis' and Mum called 'God, here we go again!'

My grandad's not the cuddly sort who gives sweets to his grandchildren and reads them bedtime stories, nor is he like Rebecca's grandad, who's young and hip. But he's the only grandparent I've got, so I try to make the best of it. He lives round the corner from us in Ship Street, and his greatest claim to fame – unfortunately for us – is that he manages to cause havoc in the lives of everybody who knows him.

I don't mean to be unkind, but that's what he does. He's always rowing with the neighbours and having to be sorted out, and setting things on fire by accident, and getting himself locked out. He says that he's too old to live alone, but Mum says men of twice his age are living on their own and making a good job of it.

She's exaggerating, of course, but we don't have room for him at our house, and Jane – who does have room – refuses to have him because she says he'd drive her nuts.

I know what she means, but I do feel sorry for him. I try to like him, but it's difficult. He's the sort of man who proudly describes his favourite hobby as writing letters of complaint. Supermarkets, train companies, the government, his neighbours, the local church, the local school, the National Parks Authority – they all know what I'm talking about. In fact, the word round town is that Grandma died just to get away from him.

People say it as a joke, but she could have done, you know. She was too young to die – everybody said that – and all she had was diabetes. It happened ages ago now but, as far as Grandad was concerned, it could have been last week. He went on about it all the time, blaming everybody from the doctors to the woman who brought round the Meals on Wheels, as if the whole thing was a plot to ruin his life. Mum said she was surprised he hadn't written a letter of complaint to God. But he probably had done, knowing Grandad.

Mum also said that he and Grandma brought it on themselves with their diet, eating all those sweets and fatty foods. She should have known better than to say that around a hypochondriac like me. My fears for my health flared to panic proportions and I swore I'd never eat another cream cake. After that, I'd lie awake at night worrying about whether diabetes was hereditary, and spent my days researching on the Internet, looking up other diseases too, like obesity, blocked arteries and cancer of the small intestine, which could all result from eating too much butter, sugar or white bread.

It was hard to know what was safe. Every article I found ran a different scare story. Either it was the chemicals that were endangering me, or the fat content, or the lack of fibre, causing cancer, or too much of it, causing something else – I can't remember what.

In the end, I gave up in confusion and swore I'd never read another article. Things returned to normal – by which I mean I stopped researching diabetes and started eating what I liked. Life was too short, I reckoned, to never eat what I wanted – which was probably what Grandma reckoned too, but, oh well.

I also made a conscious effort to live life to the full and to put to death my killer streak of hypochondria. To this end, it helped to avoid Grandad – something that was difficult because he lived so close. Poor old Grandad. He hated living on his own and hated 'doing for himself'. Mum tried to help him, but it made no difference. The more she called on him, the more he grumbled, and the more he grumbled, the madder she got.

Then, one Saturday afternoon, Mum came home

from Ship Street, tossed off her shoes, flung herself into her favourite armchair and said, 'You'll never guess what he's saying now.' *He* was always Grandad.

'What?' we said.

'He says he's getting married,' Mum said.

The house erupted. Dad whooped. Kate burst out laughing. I came rushing in from the other room. Even Lizzie ran in from the garden and leapt about barking. Mum phoned Jane, who came down the road with Imogen Louise, not wanting to miss out on the family conference.

Grandad had made a friend, it seemed – Mrs Morris, from down on the seafront, whose husband had died a few months ago. She had a nice big Victorian house with views over Newport Bay, and some money behind her. She looked a bit like Grandma, apparently, and was even the same size as her, which, according to Grandad, meant she'd fit into Grandma's clothes and he wouldn't have to throw them away.

Grandad hated throwing things away, and he loved women who were tidy, clean and house-proud, good cooks, careful with money and respectful of his opinions. This was why he'd hit on Mrs Morris. She was all those things, apparently. A real treasure, and someone who could be guaranteed to give him back his quality of life – especially if he sold his house and moved into hers and banked the profits!

Research

'I don't *believe* it,' Jane said, her tone of voice reflecting exactly our sense of shock.

'Yuck!' Kate said.

'He thinks he's getting Grandma back.' This from Dad.

'What does Mrs Morris think about it?' I said.

'She doesn't think anything,' Mum replied. 'She doesn't know. He hasn't asked her yet. Before he goes ahead, he wants our blessing.'

'He wants our *what*?' Jane said. 'You mean it's up to *us*?'

Mum nodded. We looked round at each other in a state of shock. I think it was then that Dad coined the phrase 'The Grandad Crisis'. *What were we to do?* On the one hand, we could make Grandad happy by giving him our blessing, in the certain knowledge that Mrs Morris didn't have a clue what she was letting herself in for. Or we could stop the whole thing before it ever took off – and prevent a lonely man from finding comfort in his final years.

Everybody had an opinion and, of course, they were all different. Jane said that Grandad was depressed and needed crystal therapy. Mum said that what he needed was to think about others for a change and not only himself. Dad said he needed sex, and who could blame him, the old dog. He also said it wasn't up to us and we should refuse to either give our blessing or not.

Kate said that he should marry, but she only said it because she wanted to get him off our hands. And I said, 'What about love?' This was something that nobody had mentioned. If Grandad really loved Mrs Morris, it seemed to me that he should go ahead and marry her.

The worry, however, was that he didn't.

In the end, I decided to go round and see Grandad for myself, and try to find out what *he* felt. Everybody was talking *about* him but nobody was listening *to* him. I went round and tapped on the back door. I could hear him whistling inside, which had to be a good sign. But, by the time he opened up, his face was long and sad, and he was dabbing at his eyes with the corner of his handkerchief. He was obviously putting it on in order to get sympathy.

'I hear you want to get married,' I said, feeling rattled and not caring if I showed it.

Grandad looked taken aback. He came from a generation that didn't talk about things like that in front of children. 'Did your mother tell you that?' he said.

'She didn't need to. It's all over Newport,' I said, somewhat cruelly but I couldn't help myself.

Grandad went bright red.

'Only joking,' I added quickly. 'Nobody knows – only us. Mum says you want our blessing, so I thought I'd come and hear all about it.'

Research

Grandad invited me in. He poured me a glass of orange squash in a kiddies' Mickey Mouse cup, and we went and sat in the conservatory and looked at the last few apples hanging in his garden. Grandma's favourite *Music from the Classics* record droned mournfully in the background, and Grandad started talking about her. Poor old Mrs Morris never got a look-in.

'Your grandmother was a saint,' he said. 'We never had a cross word in forty-eight years. Our marriage was perfect, Elin. *It was perfect.* I knew she was the one for me the moment I set eyes on her. She was the prettiest girl I'd ever seen. She had the face of an angel, and she was tidy too. She knew how to keep herself spick and span, not a speck on her shoes, not a hair out of place.

'It was the same in the house. Everything always had to be just so. Your grandmother was a hard little worker. I never had to do a thing for myself. My tea was always on the table on the dot of six, and everything was done to clockwork. I never had to ask. It was always there.

'Every morning, when I got up, a new shirt would be starched and ironed, waiting for me. I used to look so smart. Every day for forty-eight years, I looked smart. Your grandmother even ironed a shirt for me the day she died – and you can't say that for many women.'

You couldn't indeed. Suddenly I saw Mum's arguments with Dad on the subject of ironing in a whole new light!

'Your grandmother was a woman in a million,' Grandad carried on. 'Routine was her key. On Mondays she'd be up early doing the washing and it would be hanging out to dry by the time I got up. On Tuesdays she'd iron the sheets, change the beds, clean the bedrooms and do all the mending. On Wednesdays she'd clean the windows, inside and out, and do the main week's shopping. And she'd carry it all home as well – she wasn't like you modern women, who can't do a thing without a car. On Thursdays she'd do the bathroom, kitchen, hall and front garden. She also went to the mobile library and changed our books. On Fridays she did the back garden, and I helped her, because it's nice for a man to help his wife. On Saturdays she baked while I watched the football on the telly. On Sundays she made a big roast dinner while I went to the pub.'

He beamed at me. Poor old Grandma, I thought!

'Same with our meals,' Grandad said. 'Order ruled the day. Mondays, shepherd's pie. Tuesdays, casserole. Wednesdays, a nice piece of chicken or a lamb chop. Thursdays, steak pie. Fridays, fish. Saturdays, sausages. Sundays, the roast of course. Now she's gone, Meals on Wheels bring round anything, on any old day. I never know what's coming next.'

He started crying again. Later, I asked Mum if their lives had really been like that and, when she said they had, I asked her how she'd stuck it.

Mum laughed. 'There's no answer to that,' she said, 'but in case you haven't noticed, I've lived my life in a state of rebellion ever since!'

She also said that life had been like that for lots of people in those days. It wasn't only Grandad and Grandma who'd lived that way. I said it sounded like slavery, but Mum said that Grandma had gone along with it. She could have stood up for herself, but she never did.

After that, my marriage project lost some of its lustre. 'We were one in heart and mind,' Grandad had said as I left that afternoon, and he meant it as the highest compliment.

But that night in bed, I thought about his words. Was that what I really wanted, I asked myself? To stop being me and be a part of someone else? I tossed and turned and couldn't sleep. Where was my research getting me? For all my hard work, I felt no closer to understanding what made men tick. And I wasn't sure I wanted to either – not after spending time with Grandad!

late again
rushed
unprepared

HANGOVER!

Part II
Hard Graft

Queen of My Castle

Dr Right Monsieur le Comte de

Danger
Keep out

4

Monsieur le Comte de Dr Right

At school, my grades had slipped to a worrying degree and my teachers couldn't understand why. I'd always done so well, but now some of them wondered if, because my birthday fell on the last day of the academic year, I wasn't ready yet for GCSE work. They suggested I didn't have the maturity and might need mentoring to help me through. Some blamed Lucy's death, even though she hadn't been one of my personal friends, and some even wondered if my sudden loss of form meant that there was 'something wrong at home'.

I knew this for a fact because Mum went to yoga with my German teacher, Miss Hoskins, and she said that there were even mutterings about referring me to an educational psychologist, or getting a doctor to check my general health. I knew I'd been spending too much time on my Mrs Marridge Project, but I hadn't realized things were *that* bad. There'd been a Maths test that I'd mucked up, when I should have passed it standing on my head, and German wasn't exactly my favourite subject, but I hadn't realized I had anything serious to worry about.

I tried to say as much to Mum, but she was too angry at the suggestion that home might be to blame to listen to a word I said. By the time she'd finished going on, I was pretty angry too. I retired to my bedroom, yelling, 'Whose education is it anyway – yours or mine?' to which Mum replied, 'Mine, as long as I'm paying for it!'

I couldn't sleep that night. My head throbbed and, even in the darkness with the curtains tightly drawn, I had lights flashing in front of my eyes. They started in the corners and worked their way in until my vision was full of them. Nothing like this had ever happened to me before and I put a warning asterisk in my diary next to the words 'AN ALARMING NEW SYMPTOM'.

The situation wasn't helped by Mum and Dad, in bed next door, discussing my education loudly enough for the whole road to hear. According to Mum, the only reason I was flunking school was to get at her because I had this awkward streak and always had to wind her up. But according to Dad, it was no time at all since Lucy Chan's funeral and a fall-off in work was only to be expected. Mum eventually conceded that he might be right – but that didn't stop her going on at me the next day.

'You do know, don't you, that the sky's the limit for girls like you?' she said over breakfast. 'The opportunities nowadays are extraordinary. Girls can become anything they want to – chief executives, professors, doctors, solicitors – you name it, they can do it. And it all starts here, Elin. It all starts now. You've got to make it happen. Right here, right now. It's up to you.'

If Mum was on a mission to inspire, it failed miserably. That day in school, I daydreamt wildly of another life where tests and deadlines no longer hung over me. My friends commented on how quiet I seemed, and so did Mum when I got home.

'Why won't you answer when I speak to you?' she said as I turned my back on her and headed for my room.

'I haven't got the time,' I muttered. 'I'm too busy, right here, right now, making it happen. That's what you want, isn't it?'

Mum didn't hear me, but I still felt as if I'd scored a point. It didn't make me feel any better, though. I flung myself down at my desk, knowing I should be doing my homework, but I was fed up with working for a future that didn't feel like mine. When Dad stuck his head round the door to say that it was suppertime, I said I wasn't hungry and refused to come downstairs.

Later, I heard him and Mum going on about what was wrong with me. There was no shouting this time, but I could still hear them because our house is semi-open plan, which means that sound carries everywhere. Dad started on about Lucy's death affecting both of us girls – not just Kate, but me as well.

'Kate's tough,' he said. 'She can cope. But Elin's very sensitive. She's a deep one, that girl. Once something's worked its way inside her, there's no getting it out. The more pressure she's under the worse she gets.'

I was impressed. Dad knew me better than I'd thought. He went on to say that, in his opinion, school needed to tread carefully, and so did he and Mum.

'I want her to get on too,' he said, 'just like you. But if we push too hard, who knows what damage we might do? Look, the weekend's coming up – why don't we do something nice together as a family? You know, put the homework on one side and go out somewhere?'

It was a nice idea, but I shuddered at the thought of what Dad might have in mind. Knowing him, it was bound to be educational. He couldn't help himself, and neither could Mum. It was too ingrained. Their idea of *doing something nice* would mean museums and art galleries, or a nature walk along the coast taking the binoculars to identify the wildlife.

So I started making plans of my own, sending Jenna an emergency text, looking for the perfect excuse to say no. That way, when Dad suggested a weekend's worth of family time, I'd be prepared.

'I'd love to,' I'd say, wide-eyed and innocent. 'But I've got masses of work to do for Monday, and Jenna's invited me to stay at hers so that we can get on with it together.'

It worked, as well. Dad said it was commendable to hear me sacrificing family time for work, and Mum reluctantly agreed that I could go as long as I promised to work hard and not mess around. I was thrilled, but Kate was indignant. I insisted I was only going in order to work, and she looked me straight in the eye and said, 'Pull the other leg.'

Jody and Rebecca were indignant too, because we usually did things as a foursome but, this time, only I had been invited. But I didn't care. Far from working hard together, Jenna and I planned to take her ponies on to Carningli Common and ride all day. I really liked it up there, high on the hill overlooking Newport Bay, and knew that it would be far more fun with just the two of us.

I also liked Jenna's parents. Her mother was a dentist by day – which explained why there was a pile of *Orthodontics Monthly* in their loo – and a smallholder by evening and weekend, keeping bees, goats and hens. Jenna's father helped her when he had the time, but they were her hobby, not his. He was a deputy head teacher and described himself as 'overworked and stressed'.

43

Mum said they must have loads of money, even though their house was run-down and they didn't have a TV. They had a whole stable full of horses, a boat down in the yacht club and more cars and trucks than I could count. And yet they were the friendliest people in the world. They never made you feel beneath them, like Rebecca's father, who thought he was the king of the town because he lived in a hacienda-style bungalow with a swimming pool. Rebecca's house felt like a showcase, but Jenna's always felt like home.

On Saturday morning, Jenna walked down the track from her house to meet me, leading the ponies, and we rode all the way back, talking and laughing and having a good time. Jenna was my newest best friend, having only moved into the area the year before, but, if I was honest with myself, I felt closer to her than to either Jody or Rebecca.

She was always there for me, texting even when I didn't bother to text back, and listening to what I had to say instead of talking about herself all the time, like some people I could mention, Rebecca Edwards! On the way up the track, I told her about the school's threat to mentor me, and we agreed that teachers were mad. I also told her about the flashing lights in front of my eyes and said I was worried I might have a brain tumour.

Jenna laughed. She knew all about my health fears. 'Girls our age don't get things like that,' she said.

44

'Are you sure?' I said. 'I thought I might be dying.'

'The only way you're going to die is if you have a freak accident,' Jenna said.

Could I possibly have a freak accident today? Carningli Common opened out before us and I decided it simply wasn't possible – not when life suddenly felt so good. After that, I didn't give my health another thought. We rode the ponies until we were exhausted, and they probably were too, climbed trees and made dens as if we were little kids. It was a great day. We sunbathed on rocks that were as warm as if it were still summer, and not once did we give a moment's thought to school work.

Finally, we rode back to Jenna's house and made ourselves at home in the bunkhouse over the stable, where we cooked a meal and did things with our hair. Jenna's frizz got straightened and my dead-straight hair was given the curling-tongs treatment. Jenna's older brother, Rhys, laughed his head off when he saw us. I hadn't even known that he was home, but suddenly he appeared, standing in the doorway shaking his head.

'What a crazy pair you are!' he said. 'Just look at you. The grass is always greener on the other side!'

I didn't mind Rhys teasing because I could tell he meant no harm. If I'd had a brother, I'd have wanted one just like him. He came in and helped us rearrange the bunkhouse to make it cosier, shifting furniture and hanging our posters on the walls. It was the first chance to get to know him, because he was mostly away at university. I watched him with sharp interest. Ever since my afternoon with Grandad, my Mrs Marridge Project had been on hold, but now I felt a stirring of interest again.

'Why does your brother wear a gold ring on his engagement finger?' I asked, after he had gone.

Jenna rolled her eyes. 'Because he's engaged,' she said.

'But boys don't wear engagement rings,' I said.

'Rhys does,' Jenna answered.

'You never told me he was engaged,' I said.

'I'm sure I did,' said Jenna. 'It's just you never listen. You've always got your head in the clouds.'

She was probably right, but I was listening now – and I wanted to know more. Rhys was the first person anywhere near me in age who'd ever decided to get married. What did Jenna's parents think about it, I demanded to know? And how had Rhys realized that he'd found the right girl for him? When was the wedding going to take place, and could I go along and watch – you know, slip in at the back, or something like that? And was a baby was on the way, or did they want to get married anyway?

Jenna said they wanted to get married anyway, and it would be hard to slip in at the back as Rhys's bride-to-be, Marika, came from Finland, where she and Rhys had met on a college cultural exchange. This fired my imagination even more. But before I could ask any further questions, Jenna's mum came in to check that we had settled down for the night and had everything we needed.

We assured her that we did, and she turned out the light, extracting promises from us – on pain of death – that we'd stay in bed till morning and wouldn't talk all night. Then she left us to our own devices.

Almost immediately, Jenna curled up with her back to me, as if to say she'd had enough of questions and wanted to go to sleep. It had been a long day and who could blame her? I listened as her breathing grew deeper and slower, wishing I could sleep as well, but my mind was full of Finland, wondering what its wedding customs were like, and feeling – for the first time since my terrible afternoon with Grandad – as if I actually had something to work on.

I wished I had a notebook with me and could write things down. The moon shone through the window, big and full, lighting up the posters on the walls around me. Some were of mountain views with mottoes under them saying things like 'Peace is an Empty Mountain Top' and 'Cherish Life'. But others were of boy bands that Jenna and I fancied.

I knew their faces off by heart, but now I looked at them again with the eyes of a researcher whose subject was 'Men'. What clues were in those faces, waiting to be unlocked? Was it possible, at a glance, to distinguish between the potentially good husbands and the no-hopers? Was it in their eyes, or mouths, or the lines of their chins? Or was it all down to chemistry? Would you feel in your bones when you encountered Mr Right? And, if so, how exactly did *that* work?

The boys stared back at me, their eyes full of secrets, impossible to fathom. There were thousands of girls out there, I knew, who were convinced that one or other of those boys was the love of their life But how were they supposed to tell if what they felt was the real thing or just a crush?

I sighed at the difficulty of the task, and Jenna turned over, much to my surprise, and said, 'I can't sleep either. Are you cold? Do you need another blanket? What are you thinking about over there?'

I wished that I could tell her, but there was something about the Mrs Marridge Project that I knew I couldn't talk about to anyone.

'I'm thinking about my GCSEs,' I said. 'And what I want to do when I leave school. What about you? What do *you* want to be?'

Jenna half sat up, resting her head on her hand. She thought about it for a minute, then said, 'When people ask me that, I tend to say a jockey because they know I love horses, and it's more or less what they expect.

But the truth is that I've grown too tall for anything like that and nobody's ever heard of what I really want to be.'

'What's that?' I said.

'A hydro-geologist,' Jenna said.

'A hydro-*what*?' I asked her

'See what I mean?' Jenna said. 'A hydro-geologist is someone who goes to places like Indonesia for aid agencies, and digs wells and brings clean water to refugees.'

'You mean, you think you're going to save the world?' I said.

'Don't mock,' Jenna said, 'because the last laugh could well be on you when I meet some gorgeous Médecins Sans Frontières doctor in a refugee camp somewhere, and we work together night and day, and fall deeply in love.'

'I wouldn't get too excited if I were you. You'll probably die together in a hail of gunfire on some mercy mission, struggling to get the aid through,' I said.

'Then you'll feel ashamed of yourself for laughing at a pair of the world's great humanitarians, not to say anything of its greatest lovers,' Jenna said.

'What a waste to the world.'

'But terribly romantic.'

We burst out laughing. I said our imaginations might just be running away with us, and Jenna conceded that they mightn't actually die together, but she reckoned that they'd live out the rest of their lives in a beautiful French château, because her dashing doctor would be a comte as well.

I asked how she'd know he was her Monsieur le Comte de Dr Right, and she said, 'That's easy. It's the least of my worries. All I have to do is find some church at full moon, walk round it seven times anticlockwise and then I'll see my future husband on the final stroke of midnight. Haven't you ever heard that one?'

I said I hadn't and we laughed again, and agreed that superstitions like that were ridiculous. But the moon was bright on the bunkhouse wall, and the clock said twenty past eleven, and suddenly the two of us were out of our sleeping bags and into our clothes, giggling our heads off and convinced that, if we hurried, we could get down to the nearest churchyard before the final stroke of midnight.

We couldn't have managed it without the ponies. We led them out of the yard and down the track, kicking them into action when we were out of sound of the house, so that they galloped all the way to the churchyard. We arrived with time to spare – or so we thought, until we started counting out our circuits!

You wouldn't believe how long it took to walk round seven times – plus an extra two, because the first two laps were performed clockwise instead of anticlockwise and we had to start again. But we did it in the end, panting and laughing, not expecting to see anything, but terrified in case we did. The church clock duly tolled twelve times. On the tenth stroke, Jenna saw a cat. On the eleventh, I saw a drunk wending his way home from the Golden Lion Hotel.

And, on the twelfth, we saw an ambulance hurtling up the road towards Carningli Common – heading for the track to Jenna's house.

5

The Hands-on Approach

Jenna's father had had a heart attack. I'd been dimly aware that he had some sort of health problem which had been the cause of their moving to the peace and quiet of Carningli Common. Aware, too, that he sometimes put little pills under his tongue. But I'd never known why, not until now.

By the time we returned to the house, it was too late for little pills. The ambulance had rushed him away and Jenna's mother had gone too, leaving Rhys behind to wait for us and tell us what had happened. Jenna wept with guilt for having broken her promise to stay in bed till morning. She felt to blame because she'd made her promise on pain of death. Rhys told her not to be so silly – their father's illness wasn't her, or anybody else's, fault and there was no saying that he would die anyway. But Jenna wasn't convinced.

Afraid of being in the way, I offered to go home. But Rhys suggested I stay the night to keep Jenna and him company. We brought our sleeping bags and blankets in from the bunkhouse and bedded down, all three of us, in the living room right next to the phone. None of us could sleep and we talked about all sorts of things that night. In the dark, we shared our secrets with each other – but I still didn't say anything about my marriage project.

In the morning, the news from the hospital was encouraging. Jenna's mum came home talking about 'warning shots across the bows' and the possibility of Jenna's dad being home before too long, if things continued to go well.

She drove me back to Goat Street, then the three of them carried on to the hospital together. I thought about them all day, wondering how they were getting on. It was a funny, restless sort of day. Yet again, the unpredictability of life had reared its ugly head and shocked me. It was full of surprises. You never knew what was lurking around the next corner.

This provided me with an added incentive to get on with my marriage project. Anything could happen, I thought. You never knew what to expect next. Besides, my schoolteachers were always going on about the next two years passing in a whirl and it being impor-tant not to slacken.

In this frame of mind, I set to work in earnest, writing up everything Jenna had said about Rhys and Marika's romance, and researching Scandinavian wedding customs on the Internet. But I was moving too slowly, and I knew it. If I wanted to end up marching down the aisle in two years' time, I needed to research 'Men' in a far wider social context and get sharper and more focused.

It wasn't good enough to simply write about my family and friends. There was a whole world of men out there, waiting to teach me things I didn't have a clue about, and I had to get out there and meet them.

To this end, I bought myself a notebook and promised I'd never go anywhere without it. On the bus, on the street – everywhere I went – I'd watch what men were doing and write it all down.

I also devised a questionnaire that I handed out in Fishguard while everybody else in my class handed out Geography questionnaires. Theirs came back with information about traffic flow, car-park arrangements and access for the disabled. But mine came back with information that I hoped would prove invaluable in my hunt to find a husband.

It made depressing reading, though. What I'd asked was what men thought about marriage – whether they'd recommend it or not, what they looked for in a wife and what they thought about true love. But perhaps the men I'd questioned hadn't taken the subject seriously enough. Either that, or they were teasing me when they wrote, 'Marriage is fine – but not for me',

'Be warned – it's not worth the cost of the buttonhole' and 'The sex is memorable for five minutes and forget-table for the next fifty years.'

Perhaps I'd handed out the questionnaires to the wrong men. Or perhaps it was the men of Fishguard who were wrong. Or perhaps all men were wrong and needed women to put them right. There was obviously a lot about men that I could do with finding out. What I needed, I decided, was practical experience. Question-naires were all very well, but nothing beat the Hands–on Approach.

But how I was going to achieve this, I'd no idea – until an invitation arrived to Rebecca's birthday-party sleepover. Since the age of three, her birthday parties had always been the highlights of my social calendar, but this year Mum wasn't so keen on letting me go.

'All that girl thinks about is boys,' she said. 'I don't know what's got into her. These days, she doesn't seem to have a brain in her head. I blame the parents, I really do. There's *no way* I'd let you sleep over at their house. Don't even think about it.'

As far as Mum was concerned, that was the end of the conversation. But it wasn't the end for me. There was no way that I was going to miss the opportunities presented by Rebecca's invitation.

But how to change Mum's mind?

I decided to come at the problem laterally. Word had

reached home from school that my grades were still bad and Mum was furious. This was something, I decided, that could be turned to my advantage.

'What would you pay me if my grades improved?' I said one afternoon, initiating a conversation that was dangerous, to put it mildly, but I had a plan and reckoned I could pull it off.

Mum eyed me coldly. 'I'd love it if your grades improved,' she said, 'but I wouldn't pay you anything. You know that. I don't believe in paying. I believe in study for its own sake.'

'But that's not fair,' I said. 'Everybody else gets paid. I'm the only one who doesn't. Jody gets a pound for every good mark she brings home, and her parents are going to pay her five pounds for every A grade in her end-of-year exams, and ten for every GCSE. And as for Rebecca's parents . . .'

Mum snorted at the very mention of Rebecca's parents, who, in her opinion, had more money than sense. 'I don't care what other parents do,' she said. 'I do what's right for you and, if your grades improve, I'll give you *something*. I don't know what, but it won't be money, so don't expect it.'

Poor old Mum – I'd got her exactly where I wanted her, and she didn't even know it! From that point onwards, I temporarily put aside the Mrs Marridge Project and transferred my efforts to my school work.

It's amazing what you can do when you set your mind to it. By the weekend of Rebecca's party I had a string of 'Well done's in my homework diary and my grades were on the up.

I showed my books to Mum the night before the party and she looked impressed. So impressed, in fact, that when I mentioned the subject of a reward, she laughed and said, 'All right. You win. What do you want – and don't say money!'

'I want to go to Rebecca's party,' I said, quick as a flash. 'And I want to sleep over like the other girls. The whole class is going and I don't want to be the only one left out.'

Mum looked at me as if she knew she'd walked into a trap. 'You can't do that. It's out of the question. You *know* you can't. I don't know why you're even suggesting it,' she said.

'I know that if I don't my grades will slip again,' I said.

Mum laughed, as if she wanted to believe that I was only joking. And I laughed too, as if I hadn't meant to threaten her – oh no, I'd never do a thing like that. But I knew I'd won.

Next evening, Mum drove me down to Rebecca's bungalow and dropped me at the gate with my things packed in an overnight bag. I was hours early for the party, but she didn't know that. She waved goodbye, and Rebecca's parents stood on the front step waving back. But no sooner had Rebecca and I gone to her room, giggling our heads off and full of secret plans, than her parents were out of the house. Each went their separate way with plans of their own, blithely unaware that their angel daughter had anything organized behind their backs.

They were like that, Rebecca's parents. Against all evidence to the contrary, they thought that she was perfect. As soon as they had gone, however, she was rolling up the rugs, hiding all the ornaments, hanging fairy lights across the patio and around the empty swimming pool, and putting joss sticks everywhere to mask the smell of cigarette smoke. I helped her drape the furniture with old sheets and together we lined up her secret stash of booze. Then Jody arrived and the three of us got dressed. Rebecca said my taste in clothes was appalling and I'd have to borrow some of hers.

This was fine by me, as her wardrobe was impressive. I could have spent for ever choosing, but finally I settled on hip-hugging jeans and a black halter top, greatly enhanced by an under-wired bra, padded out with handkerchiefs because I had precious little else to give me shape. Then Jody did my hair, and Rebecca did my make-up, insisting that she was doing her best but there wasn't much hope with a face like mine.

After we'd finished insulting each other, we went into the kitchen to heat up frozen party snacks. Jody sorted out the music while Rebecca started greeting her guests. In no time at all, most of the class was there, including a grumpy-looking Jenna, who'd have to leave early because her parents didn't know where she was. Half the boys in town were there, as well as half the boys from Fishguard. Jody said she didn't know how Rebecca had managed it, but Jenna said that it was obvious – you only had to look at her.

Once Rebecca had been as mousy-brown as the rest of us, but recently a new Rebecca had been born, following a London weekend with her mother, at the end of which they had both returned with blonde hair. Since then, nothing had been quite the same. Blondes really *did* have more fun, it seemed. Boys clustered round Rebecca like wasps round a Coke can. They couldn't keep away. Her mobile was always going off in the classroom, getting her into trouble. She hardly ever did any work, but she said it didn't matter because she was going to leave school at sixteen and become a supermodel.

The teachers said that even supermodels needed an education and they weren't as dumb as Rebecca might think. In fact, most of them were very bright and, when all that money started rolling in, they thanked God for their Maths GCSE. But Rebecca wasn't listening. She was too busy having a good time, living life at twice the speed as the rest of us.

I was sure that she was boasting half the time when she talked about the places she'd been, the things she'd done and the boys she'd done them with. But, watching her now, I wasn't so sure. She was so confident. So certain of herself. Jody was prettier than her, and Jenna far more interesting, but, next to Rebecca, they faded into insignificance.

We all did. None of us stood a chance. As if they hadn't realized yet, the other girls competed for the boys' attention. But I wandered off, feeling sorry for myself. If the rest of them couldn't get a look-in, what hope was there for me and my Hands-on Approach?

I decided to have a drink. There was certainly plenty available — wine and beer, an assortment of spirits and an exotic-looking punch that Rebecca had mixed up. I'd never drunk much before — just glasses of wine on family occasions — but what else was there to do?

I tucked in with gusto, trying anything that I could lay my hands on. In no time at all, I didn't care that Rebecca was a million times more attractive to boys than anybody else and had all their attention. Music was playing, so I began to dance. I had no one to dance with, but I didn't care about that either. I drank as I danced, swigging from a bottle and swaying in rhythm to the music – a clever balancing act that I managed to keep going for most of the evening. The more I drank, the less I felt like me, and the less I felt like me, the happier it made me.

All around the room, boys started watching me. They turned from Rebecca and stared at me instead. I couldn't quite believe it, but they did. I drank more, and danced harder, shaking and gyrating, feeling strangely powerful. Boys started coming up and wanting to dance too. I thought they'd discovered that I was the most interesting girl in the room. Never for a moment did it occur to me that they might be laughing at me or trying to take advantage.

I drank and drank, and danced and danced, and sat on knees, and held boys tight and felt the world go round. Then, at some point in the evening, I started making out. I can't remember who with, or how it started, or how many boys I actually snogged, because somewhere in the evening my memory started blurring.

All I know is that I snogged on the dance floor, and snogged in the bathroom, snogged on the patio and even snogged in the empty swimming pool. The only thing that stopped me, as I remember it, was being sick. I brought up the contents of my stomach on Rebecca's parents' carpet, and Jody had to clear it up because I couldn't do it myself. Then she and Jenna put me to bed, and that was the end of boys.

I remember lying staring up at the ceiling, feeling ghastly but unable to stop laughing. A whole new life had opened up for me. Suddenly I felt like a true woman. 'I'll never forget tonight,' I swore. 'Never forget a single detail.' But I did.

Next day, I could hardly remember a thing. I woke up with a massive headache and couldn't work out why. Half of what had happened was forgotten, and probably would be to this day if a grim-faced Rebecca hadn't told me all about it in great detail. I'd made an utter fool of myself, according to her. I'd been the butt of everybody's jokes. The talk of the whole party.

It was the same at school on Monday morning. I walked into the classroom and everybody fell silent as if I'd been the only topic of conversation. I could have died. The way they looked at me you'd have thought I was the class slapper. Jody stuck up for me and so did Jenna. But Rebecca was furious with me, and told everyone who'd listen – and that was *everyone* – that I'd ruined a five-thousand-pound carpet, and got her massively into trouble with her parents, and now she never wanted to speak to me again.

By the time the day was over, I couldn't wait to get home. But first I had to face the boys. I hurried past the wall where they all sat waiting for the girls to come out of school, not daring to imagine what they might be thinking of me. On the bus home, I was sure that I could hear them laughing. I sat with my head down, refusing to look at anyone and swearing I'd never touch another drop of alcohol for the rest of my life.

I wrote this in my diary when I got home, putting a huge asterisk in the margin to mark the size of my hangover, which I swore I still hadn't quite shaken off. Then I got out my Mrs Marridge Project box file and sat with it unopened in front of me. I had a choice, it seemed. Either I could give up, assume I'd blown my chances with the opposite sex and never think about marriage again. Or I could carry on regardless – find that little bit of ice inside my heart that marked me out as a true campaigner and turn the whole experience on its head.

I sat for ages, knowing which way I'd like to go but not if I had the courage to go through with it. Getting drunk at Rebecca's party definitely hadn't been a part of the plan, and now I wondered what else was out there, if I carried on, lying in wait to humiliate me. There was so much still to do, but was it worth all the hassle? Wouldn't it be better to opt for the easy path in life and get on with my school work, like everybody else, go to university and make my parents pleased with me?

That night, I lay awake for ages, trying to decide

what to do. 'All that trouble,' I thought, 'all that pain – is getting married really worth it?'

I didn't know. But one thing was for sure – *I'd had enough of researching 'Men'!*

6

Queen of My Own Castle

Half-term arrived, bringing with it a welcome break from school. Mum and Dad were out at work all day, and Kate had gone off for a few days with Lucy Chan's family, so that left me in the house alone.

I liked it that way. It gave me time to think. I spread the Mrs Marridge Project out on my bed and knew that there was no way I could give it up. I had to carry on, no matter what a mess I'd made of 'Men'. There were other things I could research, I told myself. Marriage wasn't only about husbands. It was about all those other things on my research list – nice, safe, easy things like 'Babies', 'Property Prices' and 'DIY'.

Not caring much for babies or DIY, I decided to spend my half-term researching house prices. After all, if I was going to get married I'd need a home, and I didn't have a clue how to get one or how much it was likely to cost. To this end, I dug out all the property pages in the local newspaper, cutting out everything that caught my eye.

I came up with farms and smallholdings, country cottages and mansions, smart town houses and even a couple of derelict castles that I knew I couldn't possibly ever afford. But there was no harm in dreaming – at least, that's what I told myself.

As the file grew, however, my dreams began to fade. Not even the smallest, most derelict cottage in our area was remotely affordable for a young married couple starting out in life. Our little house in Goat Street was worth a bomb, if the properties pages were to be believed. Rebecca's bungalow would make her parents millionaires, and even Grandad's terraced house on Ship Street would make him wealthy, as would Jane's one-up-one-down.

I went down to the local estate agent's, to see if it was the same there. The windows were full of photographs of pretty stone cottages with roses growing round their doors, but even the smallest of them was beyond the means of ordinary people, or so it seemed to me.

'It isn't fair,' I thought. 'What are people who need homes supposed to do?'

I turned away in disgust, but something caught my eye in the side window where the agents showed properties that they weren't quite so proud of. In this case, you could quite see why. Unlike the pretty properties in the front window, the one I looked at now was in a terrible state. The blurb described it as 'prime building land, with planning permission', but the photograph showed a wilderness of brambles and a broken-down old clapboard house on stilts. Verandas ran round three sides of it and signs hung from it saying DANGER – KEEP OUT. All the windows were empty and a couple of them were broken. But the house over-looked the estuary and something about it captured my imagination, so I decided to go and take a look.

It was a long tramp out of town and the house took ages to find, but it was worth the effort when I finally arrived. I pushed my way through bramble bushes and found that it was smaller than I'd expected, but impos-sible not to fall in love with. It was completely on its own, right at the top of the estuary, where the wind lashed in from the ocean with no trees to stop it.

It was every bit as run-down as the estate agent's blurb had suggested, but its windows were full of light and its view of the estuary – with the sea rolling in to meet it – was sensational. I climbed onto the veranda, regardless of the warning signs, and peered through all the windows, imagining curtains and pot plants, furniture and life.

It wasn't difficult to see myself in that house, sur-rounded by my possessions, with a family of my own. I walked from window to window, imagining which room would be the nursery, and which our bedroom –

whoever 'our' might be – and which the kitchen and the living room, and where on the veranda I would sit in my rocking chair, watching the tides going in and out, and my family growing up.

This was what I wanted, wasn't it? A place that was all my own, with nobody to nag or bother me, or make me into somebody I didn't want to be. A place as wild and lonely as an eagle's eyrie, where I could be queen of my own castle, answerable to nobody.

By the time I'd seen everything the house had to show me, it felt like mine already, and so did the life it promised. I tried to get inside, pushing on the doors, front and back, but they were all locked. Then I saw a basement door under the veranda and was just scrambling down to it when a voice yelled, 'Hey – you there, what do you think you're doing?'

Whose it was, or where it came from, I could only guess. It could have been anybody – a local farmer catching sight of me, or the estate agent bringing someone out on a viewing, or the owner maybe, fed up with kids trying to vandalize his property. I didn't wait to find out, just tore off home.

For the rest of the day, I worked on my marriage project, writing about the house and drawing plans of how I wanted it to be. Then, that evening, I watched *Changing Rooms* on the telly, followed by *Ground Force America* and a repeat of *Grand Designs*. I'd always found house make-over programmes utterly boring, but now I found them riveting.

When I went to bed that night, I got out my sketch plans and fell asleep with them propped up next to me. After that, I cut out everything that caught my eye in Mum's country living magazines, not stopping until I had a file heaving with furniture and fittings, bathroom suites, patio paving, curtains, tiled floors, oak beams, fancy kitchens, pots and pans, glass jars and ceramic vases.

I was obsessed. As research went, this certainly beat trying to understand men! I went round all the shops in Fishguard, collecting carpet samples, swatches of curtain material, brochures on dishwashers and fridges, furniture catalogues and paint colour charts. Until now, my marriage project had been hard-going, to put it mildly, but now it couldn't have been easier.

'This is much more like it,' I thought, as I researched coffee percolators, dishwasher-friendly china and the relative merits of oil, electricity or gas as a means of running a heating system.

I also decided to take up cooking. Having designed myself a light and airy kitchen with stunning views of the estuary, it seemed the most natural thing in the world to set about becoming a master chef. Mum had books from every TV cookery series you could think of sitting unused on her shelves. I worked my way through all of them, looking for the sort of meals I reckoned real men – not men like Dad, whose favourite meals were pasta and quiche – might want to eat.

Swordfish caught my attention immediately. So did Mexican Spiced Crab and Chilli Bake, Stir-fried Squid, Calves' Brains with Calvados, Orange and Whisky Coulis, and Black Forest sandwiches, made on rye bread with chocolate spread, cherries, cream cheese topping and a dash of Worcestershire sauce.

I listed all my favourite recipes under three headings – 'Foolproof', 'Gobsmackingly Delicious' and 'As Good as Fish and Chips'. I listed chef's tips under headings like 'The Dos and Don'ts of Vegetables', 'What Makes Cakes Rise' and 'How to Sharpen a Knife'. Then, when I felt ready, I started on the actual cooking, following each recipe exactly and expecting it to turn out like the photographs in the books.

But there's no such thing as foolproof, as I was to discover. Mum came home to find half her pans burned, her fridge raided, her kitchen bomb-struck and her daughter in tears. Obviously she wanted to know what was going on, and equally obviously it didn't feel like the right moment to tell her that I was preparing for married life. So I took a deep breath and told her that I was planning to apply to Jamie Oliver to train me on the telly as an apprentice chef.

This was a mistake. Mum thought I must be joking, but I insisted I was deadly serious.

'What can you be thinking of?' Mum said. 'Thank you, Jamie Oliver – thank you very much! It's not all glamour, working in a kitchen. Not a bed of roses. Not all TV cameras. It's a hard graft, unthanked for and unnoticed. Really, Elin – you can do better for yourself. Besides, you need a spark of talent to become a chef!'

We ate supper that night in grim silence – my supper, Risotto con Funghi, which looked like slugs and maggots mixed together, followed by Crème Brûlée, which should have been called Crème Noir, and almond biscuits that were as hard to bite as doggy chews. Even Dad was unimpressed – and he likes everything.

After that, I decided to give cooking a miss and have a go at DIY instead. It wasn't anything I'd ever been particularly interested in, but one of my abiding memories of Grandma was of her being unable to put up a shelf for herself, or even change a fuse in the kettle to make a cup of tea, without Grandad doing it for her. And I wasn't having that happening to me.

To this end, I passed a frustrating hour in my bedroom trying to hang shelves to house my growing marriage project. Mum and Dad didn't have a clue what was going on until I reached the drilling stage. They came rushing upstairs to see what the din was all about, and the sloping plank of wood hanging off the wall failed to impress. Not only was it wildly crooked, but half my books had slid down the back. The floor was covered in shavings and the plank in question had been bought by Dad for something else.

He pulled my handiwork off the wall – for safety's sake, he said. I protested that I could get it right if he'd only let me, but he wouldn't listen.

'I wish you'd asked before you started,' he said.

'I wish you'd put as much energy into your homework!' Mum added. 'Cookery, DIY – what'll you try your hand at next?'

There was no quick answer to that one, but it certainly wasn't homework. Despite my heroic efforts in the run-up to Rebecca's birthday, my grades had been slipping again, and Mum knew it because she'd been through my school bag. She insisted that she hadn't, but I knew that she was lying. How else would she know that my teachers had written 'Late again', 'Rushed', 'Unprepared', 'Where's the essay that you promised me last week?' and 'I asked for three *pages*, not three *lines*'.

Dad tried to keep things on an even keel, saying that he didn't want to push but I was running out of time if I didn't want to get seriously behind. You could feel the tension building up in the house. Christmas wasn't far away, followed by Kate's mocks. Mum said that Kate never should have swanned off with the Chans at half-term, and I felt sorry for her.

Kate deserved that break, if anybody did. She used to be so carefree and full of fun, but now she hardly ever smiled, and worked all the time and never talked to anyone.

'What's the point of it all?' I thought. 'I just don't get it. There's Kate – eighteen years old and in the prime of her life, and all she's got in front of her are years more slog at university, and a massive student debt to round things off. And all for what? I mean, she doesn't have a clue what she wants to be, and half the students in our town never find jobs anyway. Not if they want to live round here. For all their slog, they end up either on the dole or doing work experience for free.'

School called it *having choices*, but I called it *a trap*. We were caught, Kate and I. Our education was a waste of time. It was a game for suckers and, if Kate had never come back from her trip with the Chans, I'd have understood.

Sometimes I felt like swanning off myself.

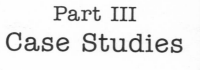

Part III
Case Studies

Last will and testament

MY DAD READS PORN !!!

Mrs ~~Marriage~~ge

Dr death.

assez toi

Assieds-toi   et fini

ton travail

Assieds-toi et finis ton travail ✓✓✓

7

Sick, Mad and Demon-possessed

It wasn't only Kate that I was worried about. I was also worried about what was happening to me. Either I was imagining it or something was definitely wrong with me. The asterisks in my diary had begun to grow, forming a distinct pattern of weariness and headaches, interspersed with buzzing sounds inside my head, dots in front of my eyes and even occasional flashing lights.

I knew these could be caused by stress but, as someone who'd always taken her medical condition very seriously indeed, I couldn't help worrying that there was more to it than that. One night, therefore – at three in the morning to be precise – I went down to Dad's computer and started researching symptoms on the Internet. This didn't help, to put it mildly. I discovered an alarming connection between headaches and brain tumours and, when I threw in buzzing sounds and flashing lights as well, I even found myself looking at schizophrenia.

Was I mad? Was that it? Certainly it would explain

my sudden obsession with getting married. Other girls my age might well dream about falling in love and marrying, but I was quite sure that none of them would ever go so far as to agonize over mortgages, fuel bills and the right way to hang shelves. They wouldn't polish up their cooking skills or research 'men' using Microsoft Excel.

No, I was definitely obsessed. Even though my school work was going downhill, I couldn't stop. I was like a person possessed.

'Sick, mad and demon-possessed,' I thought. '*Not that as well!*'

I looked up demon possession on the Internet. But it's a subject that definitely shouldn't be investigated at three-thirty in the morning, when the world is silent and dark, and it's easy to see menace in every shadow. There are websites out there, believe me, that you wouldn't want to know about.

In the end, I crept back to bed, having frightened myself so badly that I took Dad's old school Bible with me, which had lain untouched on his bookshelf for long enough to gather half a ton of dust. By next morning I felt a fool for sleeping with a Bible under my pillow, but at least I *had* slept – I could be thankful for that.

It wasn't the end of the headaches, however. In fact, I started getting stomach-aches as well, which could have been brought about by worry, but could have been a warning of something infinitely worse. By the time I'd finished researching duodenal ulcers, kidney failure and stomach cancer, I was ready to change my project title from 'Mrs Marridge' to 'Dr Death'. One way or another, I was definitely on a slippery slope. I wondered if I oughtn't to warn my family that they could well be about to lose me.

But how do you tell your family a thing like that?

In the end, I decided to run the idea past Jody and see what she thought. I chose her partly because she was good at keeping secrets and partly because her stepfather was a vet, which meant, I reckoned, that I could find out about brain tumours without having to face a regular doctor and be put through terrible tests.

I got my chance one day after school when we had her house to ourselves – apart from her little sister, Dolly, that is, and her baby brother, Jackson. Before we could talk, however, Jody had to cook tea for them because her parents were both out, and get them ready for bed. This included playing with them, bathing them, getting them into their pyjamas, reading them stories, changing Jackson's final nappy of the day and convincing them that the bogeyman wasn't about to strike the moment she tucked them in and turned out the light.

I trailed behind her, waiting for my chance to talk deep and meaningful. But by the time that Jody had read every last picture book in the house and got Dolly and Jackson off to asleep, she didn't have the energy to listen and I didn't have the energy to tell her anyway.

I was exhausted just by watching. I'd never actually witnessed Jody in action as a surrogate mum and was astonished at the calm way she handled everything. I'd scarcely dare to touch a baby for fear that it might die, but Jody hadn't batted an eyelid.

I left her slumped on the settee and walked home, glad to get a bit of peace and quiet. But if I thought I'd done with babies, I was in for a surprise. The very next evening, when I got home from school, Mum wanted to know if I could baby-sit Imogen Louise. She'd do it herself, Mum said, but she and Dad were off to Parents' Evening at school, and Kate couldn't do it because of her revision – which left only me.

'Don't worry about it, though,' Mum said. 'Jane'll understand if you're too busy. But, if you can, she says you just might save her from going nuts.'

How could I possibly say no to a request like that? Besides, I had to do something while Mum and Dad were at school, discovering how badly my work was going. And if Jody could look after a baby, *why couldn't I*?

But Imogen Louise was a different matter to Baby Jackson. He was big and bouncy and full of smiles, but she was small and quivering and, from the first time I'd set eyes on her, seemed never to have stopped crying. He appeared to like being a baby, but she obviously hated it. She was red-mouthed, gummy, hypersensitive to sound and light, furious every minute when she wasn't feeding and incapable of sleep.

Jane left her house, swearing on her life that Imogen Louise was a reformed character. But this was a downright lie. No sooner had Jane driven off, calling that I could always get her on the mobile – another lie – than a thin wail started up, growing in intensity until nothing in the world could stop it.

I tried warming up the milk left in the fridge, but Imogen Louise screamed at me and spat it out. For a baby, she had an amazing range. I checked her nappy, but it was clean. I walked up and down with her, rocking her in my arms the way that Jody had rocked Jackson, but she banged her head so violently and repeatedly against my shoulder that I feared she'd knock herself out. I tried singing to her, but that only made things worse. I tried putting her in front of the telly, but she roared at it, open-mouthed and furious.

Finally I phoned for help, but Jane's mobile was switched off. After that, in a state of despair, I sat with Imogen Louise on my lap, trying to convince myself that there was a real live person inside that tight little body and not a small red monster sent from hell. On the principle that she was enough of a person to actually have feelings, and those feelings might include likes and dislikes, I put on some of Jane's CDs.

Perhaps Imogen Louise would like Nina Simone, I told myself, or Eric Clapton, or U2, or the Beach Boys. Perhaps the sort of stuff she'd go for was Jimi Hendrix. Perhaps Handel's *Water Music* was her thing. Perhaps Norah Jones, or Eva Cassidy. Or the Doors, or Talking Heads . . .

By the time that Jane came back, I was asleep. So was Imogen Louise, curled up on my lap like a contented little kitten. It didn't seem fair to tell Jane what a terrible time I'd had, but I didn't need to – she had returned full of guilt.

'I apologize for my daughter,' she said, sliding Imogen Louise onto her own lap, plainly terrified of waking her. 'I blame it on the birth trauma. She was fine until then. A happy little baby, peaceful and contented – I just know she was. But they promised us an acupuncture home delivery and what we got instead were forceps with an epidural. It came as a terrible shock to me, and I dread to think what it did to Imogen Louise. Babies can be very sensitive. They know what's going on, even before they're born. You can talk to them, you know. Even in the womb, they understand what you're saying. I bet you didn't know that.'

I didn't. But then I'd hardly known anything about

babies until yesterday. I'd never heard of epidurals, or acupuncture home deliveries, and I wasn't sure I wanted to either. I bid a hasty retreat, thinking that I'd had enough for now. Even facing the music back at home seemed preferable.

At least, that's what I thought until I pushed open the back door, only to find that my school bag had been turned upside down and every bad essay I'd ever written tipped out on to the kitchen table. Mum and Dad looked up. They both looked pretty grim.

'Tell us, Elin,' Mum started off, as soon as I walked in. 'We can't wait to find out. What exactly have you been *doing* since school started in September – because it certainly hasn't been work, not according to your teachers, and not according to these marks.'

I glanced at Dad, hoping for a bit of sympathy. But he looked just as cross as Mum, and I guessed it wasn't the moment to initiate a conversation on whether or not I was dying. My parents wouldn't believe me. They'd think that I was making the whole thing up to get myself off the hook.

Besides, I never got the chance.

'In all my years, I've never been so embarrassed,' Mum carried on, scarcely pausing for breath. 'Your teachers are furious with your performance, and you'd think it was all our fault. They say you've let them down, and I can promise that you've let us down as well. I don't know what's the matter with you. You always manage to look busy and yet this is the result. You've got that stupid motto pinned over your desk. "Application is the Key" it says, but it doesn't make a blind bit of difference. I simply don't understand what's going on. Nobody does.'

I understood – but I couldn't explain, of course. There was no way I could tell Mum that my *stupid motto*, as she called it, had nothing to do with GCSEs – never had done and never would – and that all my busy-busy moments were being spent on the Mrs Marridge Project. I thanked God that nobody had found it yet, tucked away under my desk. It obviously wasn't safe to keep in the house any more, given all the nosing around that was going on.

I decided to take the project down to Grandad's hut for safe-keeping. The wonder was that I hadn't thought of hiding it there before. It was the perfect place because, for most of the year, nobody but me ever went down there. During the summer months, Grandad rented the hut to unsuspecting holidaymakers who didn't realize how basic it was, but during the winter months, it was vacant and I'd use it as a hideaway when things at home got on top of me. I'd sit at the window watching waves beating up the shore to the sea wall, knowing that nobody knew where I was and that was how I liked it.

The very next day therefore, after school, I sneaked the project down to the hut and stored it in a metal box under one of its beds. I found it hard to fit everything in and even harder to close the lid. Every piece of paper in that metal box represented homework that hadn't been done, tests not revised for and coursework ignored.

I almost wished my teachers could see it and know how hard I *had* been working after all. And Mum and Dad as well. But I knew I couldn't show them, because they'd never understand. I couldn't show it to a soul.

By this time it was getting dark. I left the hut, locking the door behind me, and walked home dodging waves along the sea wall. All the way, I thought about the old me, who'd always made my parents proud on Parents' Evenings, and wondered who this new me might be, who cared more for getting married than passing GCSEs.

8

On Acquiring Maturity

It wasn't only at home that I was in trouble after that Parents' Evening. During the next week, most of my teachers got me on one side for little 'chats', filling my lunch hours with good advice about what I had to do to pull myself together if I didn't want to fail my GCSEs.

My form teacher raised the subject of mentoring again. 'We know you're bright,' she said. 'But GCSEs aren't only about being bright. They're about commitment and dedication. And that requires maturity. And maturity, it seems from the way that you're behaving, is the one thing that you lack!'

That cut me to the quick. Here I was, working single-mindedly to achieve the ultimate symbol of maturity – a married status – and, in the considered opinion of my teachers, I was some child who needed leading by the hand. I raged inwardly – not least because Rebecca was doing every bit as badly as me, but nobody said that *she* suffered from immaturity.

I refused the offer of mentoring, or any other form of help. But that night, sitting in front of my bedroom mirror, staring at my stick-thin body, I despaired of ever growing up. How was I ever going to get married when I not only behaved like a child, in the eyes of those who knew me, but even looked like one too? I tried to tell myself that I was one of the lucky ones who was supermodel thin. But supermodels had breasts, not chests. They had hips, and bums, and lips, and thick, long hair and cheekbones, and legs as long and elegant as pink flamingos.

They were real women. And Rebecca was a real woman too. But I was just a child, with my baby face, scraggy hair, hipless body, lipless mouth and breasts that totally refused to grow.

Next day at school, I asked my friends how old they thought I looked.

'Oh, I'd say twelve at least,' Rebecca said, flicking back her hair.

'Would you say as old as that?' Jody said, with a wicked glint in her eye.

'You don't look any different to the rest of us. Don't listen to them. You look fourteen. What's wrong with that?' Jenna said.

If she meant to cheer me up, it didn't work. For the rest of the day, I agonized over my lack of maturity and worried about what to do. Either I could please my teachers, it seemed to me, or please myself, but there simply wasn't time for both. I could prove how grown up I was by slogging for good grades, or I could take the Mrs Marridge route, ignore the grades and work on becoming grown up in the sort of way that would find me a husband.

I fell asleep knowing that if I took the one direction Mum and Dad would never forgive me, but if I took the other I'd probably never forgive myself. It was no contest really. I mean, whose life was it anyway? In the morning I woke up knowing that the Mrs Marridge Project had won hands down. I hadn't even needed to make a choice. The night's sleep had done it for me.

After that, I felt as if I'd crossed a line. To celebrate, I filled a new file with paper and labelled it CASE STUDIES, with a sub-heading WOMEN OF MATURITY. Then I made a list of everything I needed to acquire in order to become Woman of Maturity myself. MY TOP TEN TIPS, I called them. They started, most importantly, with 1) Breasts, and worked their way through:

2) Responsibility
3) Style
4) Self-confidence
5) Good Sex
6) New Clothes

7) A Good Heart
8) Toughness
9) A Bank Account
10) Something to Do with Spirit.

I didn't know exactly what I meant by 'Heart' or, for that matter, 'Spirit'. I mean, I'm not exactly the touchy-feely type, or any more religious than anybody else – but the list seemed empty without them. Besides, what's the point of doing case studies, if not to help you discover things you don't already know?

When I'd finished, I took the list down to Grandad's hut and hid it in the metal box, along with everything else. Then I wrote out a timetable of action to take back home and give me something concrete to work towards.

And I needed that, believe me! OK, 9) was going to be easy – I mean, anyone could open up a bank account – but 1) to 8) were going to be tricky, and 10) was going to be a major challenge.

I decided to start by jumping in at the deep end, listening to Handel's *Messiah* to get me in the frame of mind for 10) while reading Bible verses on the side and doing press-ups to enlarge my chest for numbers 1), 3), 4) and 5). I also nicked a pile of my sister's magazines and started a scrapbook on the latest fashions.

Everything that caught my eye went in – even things I never would have worn myself – on the general principle that good taste rubs off and, the more you surround yourself with it, the better chance you have of becoming a Woman of Maturity.

But what made some clothes *good* and others *bad*? I didn't have a clue, if I was honest with myself, but soon my scrapbook bulged with exotic shoes, funky bags, designer sportswear, posh frocks, charity shop junk, cutting-edge labels, business chic and obscenely, dizzyingly expensive haute couture. It was growing on a daily basis. I put in everything from adverts for aftershave, worn by rain-drenched, semi-naked, gorgeous men, to photographs of supermodels frolicking in the sea, over which I drew in thought bubbles saying things like 'Watch This Spot' and 'This Could be Me'.

In no time at all, I needed to buy myself another scrapbook. But was I any closer to my chosen aim of achieving maturity? I decided to add in photographs of women who inspired me, including Jane, who mightn't have much fashion sense but dressed to please herself, no matter what anybody thought. Especially you, Carl.

This set me off on a whole new tack, and I borrowed books from the library on women who had changed the world in one way or another, in the hope that I might learn from them. The first of these wouldn't have been my natural choice, but as Dad had already bought *Marilyn in Photographs* with his birthday present tokens and was raving on about what the Monroe factor could have done for world peace, I decided to give it a go.

After I had finished − which didn't take long − I worked my way through Joan of Arc, Elizabeth I, Germaine Greer and Mother Teresa, who embodied everything on my list except for 5), but had a double helping of 10) to make up for it. Night after night I sat in my room reading up on these women, hoping that their influence would rub off on me. But I didn't feel any more mature at the end of it, and even when I put on make-up and did my hair, I didn't look any older either. When I sat in front of the mirror, painted to the nines, pouting like Victoria Beckham, it just didn't work.

Reluctantly, I decided that what was holding me back was 5), Good Sex, and that I was bound to look like a child when I had only a child's experience of life. What did I know about good sex − or any other sort of sex, for that matter? How could I hope to become a Woman of Maturity until I overcame my epic ignorance? And who was there to help me in this awesome task?

Mum, I knew, would have loved nothing better than to have nice, frank, girly, mother−daughter sex talks with me. But I would have died before I'd talk to her. And Kate would have done the same, but that would mean admitting that she knew more than me, and I'd die before I'd do that too. Then there were my friends of course, but, for all they claimed to know, my instinct said they weren't much more experienced than me.

In the end, it was Kate's magazines that I returned to. Between the tattered, cut-out pages, I found 'My Night of Passion with My Best Friend's Boyfriend', 'Undercover with the UK's Hottest Swingers' and 'How to Please Your Man – Our Top Tips, Complete with Diagrams'.

The rest I could cope with, but the Tips really did for me. Until I read them, I'd thought that sex was just a matter of starting with kisses and going with the flow. But now it seemed that there was a whole lot more to it than that. Suddenly I found myself panicking. Was this *really* what it took to please a man? If so, I didn't stand a chance!

In the end, I decided to give up on the whole thing. Sex, spirit, breasts – *everything*. What chance did I have of ever becoming a Woman of Maturity? I even wondered if a celibate marriage in single beds mightn't be a possibility. I threw away Kate's magazines, telling myself I'd lie if she asked where they were, returned the books to the library and put Dad's old school Bible back in his office.

And that was how I found his secret stash of porn!

Actually, to call it a stash is a bit of an exaggeration. After all, it was only a couple of magazines, and they were both covered in dust as if Dad hadn't looked at them for years. But it was still porn, unmistakably, hidden on the top shelf where no one ever went. I put the Bible back and a whole pile of stuff came tumbling down. I stooped to pick it up and there among the *Railway Modellers* were a pair of lurid covers filled with suntanned breasts.

I nearly died of shock. It wasn't just that breasts could be so big – which didn't help the way I felt about my own – it was the fact that my dad read porn.

My dad read porn! I grabbed the magazines as if they were hot coals, dashed upstairs with them and hurled them into the furthest corner of the room, behind my overflowing laundry basket. I should have put them back on the shelf, where no one would ever know I'd found them, but I simply didn't think. All I knew was that I never wanted to speak to that pathetic pervert, my father, again. Now I understood why Mum had never married him. *He was disgusting.*

I planned to throw the magazines away the next day. But in the morning, late for school, I forgot. In fact, I forgot for most of the day, and it was only in French after lunch that I remembered. My shock was so great that I cried out loud. Everybody turned and stared at me.

'Are you all right?' my French teacher, Mrs McAvoy, said.

I went bright red. 'I feel sick,' I said, remembering what Mum had said that very morning about sorting out my bedroom. 'I really do. You've got to believe me. I'm not making it up. *Can I go home?*'

Mrs McAvoy didn't believe me. But then she had reason not to. '*Mais non!*' she cried, having heard it all before, every time my homework was late. '*Assieds-toi et finis ton travail.*'

By the time school was over, I really *did* feel sick. Mum could be sorting out my room even now, enjoying her day off – until she found the magazines. When the school bus dropped me off, I raced home, tore upstairs and knew immediately, before I even looked behind the laundry basket, that my worst fears were about to be confirmed.

The bedroom was too tidy. My clothes had been folded and put away, my school work stacked in neat piles on my desk, my laundry basket emptied, my carpet vacuum-cleaned and my shelves dusted. I flung myself at the basket, looking in it, behind it and everywhere else too – but the magazines had gone.

'No,' I cried. '*They can't have done!*'

What was I going to do now? I broke out in a sweat. Mum would think that they were mine, and if I told her otherwise she'd turn on Dad and go ballistic. I took the whole room apart, but the magazines had definitely gone.

That night at supper, I was in a right sweat. So was Dad, or that's how it seemed to me. And so was Mum, who, I could have sworn, looked pinker than usual, and her voice just that little bit sharper. Kate looked from one of us to another, trying to figure out what was up, but I wasn't going to tell her, and nobody else was either.

After supper, I went to my room and waited for Mum to come up. I knew that after finding the magazines she'd want a 'little chat'. I sat braced for it all evening, but she never appeared. Next morning, she didn't say a word. Nor did she after school – not even when Kate went out, and she and I were alone in the house. She didn't mention anything. Not then, and not later. And neither did Dad. From that day until this, it's as if those magazines never existed.

9

The Pilgrimage

Mum may have said nothing about the magazines, but she had plenty to say about the smell of cigarette smoke on the landing in the mornings. It wasn't Dad's smoke either. It was mine. I'd only tried to smoke a couple of times – to calm my nerves, I'd told myself – but already she'd discovered it and was going on about people dying, even from a few quick puffs.

This inevitably fed my hypochondria, and I threw my cigarettes away and swore I'd never buy another pack. Brain tumours were out and lung cancer was in. There was no doubt that my chest had tightened since I'd experimented with smoking and now I reckoned that I was coughing in my sleep. I set up a tape recorder to prove my case and refused to be comforted by hours of silence.

Sometimes it's horrible being me. I always have to take things to extremes. I know I'm being silly, but I just can't stop. I suppose that's what hypochondria does to you. No sooner does the fear of lung cancer cross your mind than you're awake at night composing your Last Will and Testament. You don't want to give away your favourite things, but what else is going to happen to them when you're dead?

By the time I'd finished deciding who would have my silver locket (Mum), my diary (Jenna), my clothes (Rebecca) and my Mrs Marridge Project (Jody – on the condition that she never told a soul and burned it after reading it), I was in such a state that something drastic needed to be done. A visit to the doctor would have been the obvious option, but I decided to take a different tack and go on a pilgrimage instead.

This wasn't entirely my idea. Only a year before, Jane had been on a pilgrimage to Santiago de Compostela and came home – in her own words – *a changed woman*. According to her, pilgrimages healed the inner suffering self beneath the outward, superficial pain. I didn't have a clue what she meant by that, or by her declaration that it was the inner void that needed changing if a life was to be well lived. I knew Jane was a superstitious person, weighed down with crosses, amulets and lucky crystals, but the pilgrimage had worked for her, even curing her aches and pains, she claimed, so why not for me?

The very next Sunday morning, therefore – having explained to Mum and Dad that I was working on a case study for my local history project – I embarked on a pilgrimage of my own. Determined to do the whole thing properly, I fasted the night before and set out in typical pilgrim fashion, equipped with nothing but a walking stick.

It was a freezing, damp morning and it stayed that way all day. The path I chose wasn't hard to find because it had been a pilgrim walk for centuries, leading to the holy rock at Nevern and the churchyard beyond it, whose yews are meant to bleed with Christ's own blood. Dad wanted me to take Lizzie for the exercise and Mum wanted me to take a thermos of hot soup. But I got away without either, telling myself it wouldn't be a proper pilgrimage if I walked it any other way than hungry and alone.

It started raining as soon as I set out, which was unfortunate as my waterproofs were completely inadequate. In fact, rain fell on and off for most of the way. I tried embracing my discomfort as part of the experience, but it wasn't easy. For a good hour, the pilgrim walk followed the estuary without a single tree to shelter me. It was only after I'd entered woodland that the sun came out.

I trudged along, completely drenched, trees dripping onto me even though the rain had stopped. Long before I reached the holy rock, I was shivering with the cold and covered in mud. The path was so boggy that, even with my walking stick, I couldn't help but slip. Sometimes it was so narrow and overgrown that I had to push my way through soaking-wet bushes in order to carry on. Sometimes the trees above me hung so low that I couldn't help but get caught up, no matter how low I stooped.

By now I felt a fool for ever thinking that a walk through a muddy wood might be a way of healing inner suffering, let alone warding off lung cancer. But every time I thought about going back, something always made me carry on. It was as if a thread of silver led me through that woodland and wouldn't let me go.

It was an unforgettable day, filled with dripping trees, lonely meadows, rushing streams and winding paths lined with huge old stones half buried in moss. Not once did I hear the sound of another human voice or even a car on a road anywhere. All I heard were birds singing and running water.

I'd thought it would be difficult to feel like a pilgrim or think holy thoughts but, as I walked along, a stillness fell upon me. When the path narrowed to the width of a single foot, I knew that I was close to my destination. I scrambled over a massive tree root in the path, made my way down a steep slope – and the holy rock was right in front of me, fringed by trees.

I recognized it immediately, even though I'd never seen it before. What else could it be, with hundreds of coins and little bits of paper stuck into its every crevice?

I went and stood in front of it. It looked like some great, sad jungle beast from another age, left behind and lonely. Rain poured down it and I could feel its secret sorrow, as if all the hopes represented by those coins and notes had soaked into it and become a part of what it was.

Suddenly I wanted to do what everybody else had done – leave a coin as well, or at least a bit of paper with my name on it, so that the water of the rock could wash over it and absorb my hopes as well. I wanted to kneel where the pilgrims had knelt and offer up a prayer. But, thanks to my desire to be a proper pilgrim, I'd left everything at home. I didn't have a coin to pay for my prayer, didn't even have a piece of paper to scribble down my request.

So, in the end, I walked away. And who was to say I needed a coin anyway? Until I saw that rock, I'd thought I had everything in the world to worry about but, as I walked away, I swear I felt a lightness in my step.

I carried on down the track, reaching Nevern churchyard, where it started raining again, and I came across the first people I'd seen all day, searching for the famous 'blood' among the dusty yew trees. They asked if I'd seen it, and I said I hadn't and looked away, embarrassed, because I could have sworn the woman was crying and it wasn't just the rain running down her face. They carried on from tree to tree, locked together in some secret grief. I didn't have a clue what it was all about, but one thing was for sure — they looked far more like authentic pilgrims than me.

I left the churchyard and made my way up through the village, telling myself that my pilgrim walk was over and it was time to return to ordinary life. Nevern's a quiet little place — just a handful of cottages, a church, a village hall, a few pretty gardens dotted around a trout stream and an old pub, famous for its Sunday lunches. They were still being served as I walked past. The car park was full. Even though it was winter and the tourists had long since gone, the locals still came here. A few of them even braved the rain to sit on the pub wall, looking in the stream.

And Rebecca was one of them. She leapt up at the sight of me and called my name. It was obvious that she was desperate for company. I went over and she even admitted as much — which was quite something for her.

'I'm dying of boredom,' she said. 'It's so good to see you! Mum and Dad are driving me nuts. Come inside and I'll get them to buy you a drink. In fact, I'll get them to buy you lunch.'

After a night of fasting and nothing to eat today, Rebecca's offer was impossible to refuse. We entered the pub together, Rebecca laughing and chattering, and her parents smiling a welcome as if I hadn't ruined their carpet and cost them thousands of pounds.

All, it seemed, was forgiven. They plied me with drinks, lent me a dry sweater, asked how school was going and then ignored me – which was the way that Rebecca got treated too, so I didn't take it personally. Her father went up to the bar, 'flirting as usual', as Rebecca put it, and her mother carried on drinking heavily, saying what else could you do when your husband was 'otherwise engaged'?

Rebecca looked embarrassed. Her father was attracting the attention of the whole pub by now, trying to stick fivers down the barmaid's cleavage, and her mother was draining bottles of wine all on her own and could hardly sit up straight. Even when the lunch arrived, things didn't get much better. Poor old Rebecca – I bet she wished she'd never asked me to join her.

We ate in silence, trying to look anywhere but at her father, who point-blank refused to leave the barmaid alone. He was making a total fool of himself – but then so was she. I couldn't imagine what a girl not that many years older than me could possibly see in an old man like that. Rebecca's dad might still have his hair and waistline, but nice men didn't smile that way. Even my dad didn't smile that way, for all his secret stash of porn.

In the end, Rebecca's mother made a scene and we had to leave. She went up to the bar, hurling a look of pure hatred at the barmaid, and tried to get a bottle of vodka brought to the table. 'Put it on the slate,' she said. 'George will pay. My husband, George. You've met my husband, have you? George, my husband – the man who's stuffing fivers down your front!'

Rebecca's father frogmarched her out to his car. We all got in and drove off, me sitting rigid on the back seat, desperate not to get mud on the immaculate upholstery. It was a relief to get home. Dad might read the occasional off-limits magazine, and Mum might nag, but there were no words that day that could have described how wonderful my parents were in comparison!

That night, I wrote up Rebecca's family for my Mrs Marridge Project. It felt a bit cruel turning them into case studies, but I knew I had to do that sort of thing if I wanted to get results. I had to have a heart of ice. Where research was concerned, I couldn't allow myself to get personally involved.

I wrote down everything I could ever remember about Rebecca's parents, right back to the time when she was a bridesmaid at their wedding. It had been a magical day, blessed with sunshine. Whoever would have thought that it would come to this?

I wrote about the couple in Nevern churchyard as well, wondering who they were and what they'd been so sad about, and thinking that they mightn't have had a BMW waiting at the gate to take them home, but I reckoned I could see more love between them than Rebecca's mum and dad.

'I don't get it,' I wrote. 'Some marriages seem to work despite everything, and others have everything going for them, yet they sink like a stone. It's a mystery to me. How do you figure out which marriages will work – and can you ever be sure that your own one will be safe?'

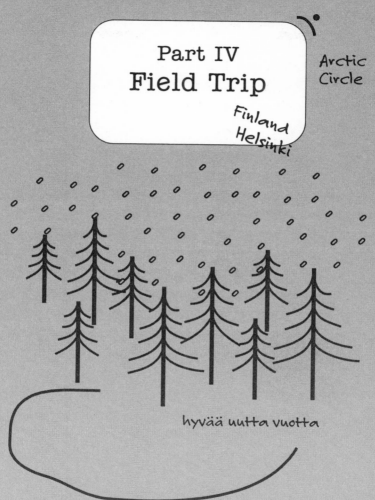

10

The Invitation

Perhaps the prayers you don't pay for get answered anyway. Who knows? Certainly it seemed that my breathing became easier after that, I stopped worrying about lung cancer and I even stopped having headaches. This could all have been a coincidence, of course, but I like to think that the pilgrimage had something to do with it.

December arrived with a sprinkling of frost that made the cliffs look as if snow had fallen. I always love winter in Newport, especially Christmas with coloured lights across the streets and the whole place buzzing and busy. Even weeks in advance, you can feel the atmosphere of anticipation. The holiday houses start filling up again and excitement's in the air.

It must have been contagious, because the pressure was suddenly off at school, which may have been another reason why I didn't have so many headaches. It was as if Christmas had got to my teachers. Peace and goodwill, and all of that. And it had got to my parents too. Suddenly they let up. Mum even stopped nagging Kate about her mocks in January. In fact, she said how well Kate was doing considering 'the Lucy thing', and how proud she was of the way she'd coped over the last few months.

Life felt good. It really did. And then it suddenly got even better! A week or so before the end of term, I went downstairs one morning to find a letter addressed to me, mixed up with all the Christmas cards on the doormat. It was an invitation to Jenna's brother Rhys's wedding. On New Year's Eve. In snow-bound Finland. Just a few miles south of the Arctic Circle.

'I can't believe you've invited me!' I said when I got Jenna on my mobile, no more than twenty seconds later.

'I don't see why. You're my best friend,' she said.

I puffed up with pride, and stayed that way all day. Jody and Rebecca hadn't been invited, and were green with envy. I knew I shouldn't gloat but couldn't help myself. Not that I knew yet if I could go. Mum's comment, when I thrust the invitation into her face, was that we couldn't possibly afford it — and it was only a marriage anyway.

'Scarcely worth travelling halfway round the globe to witness,' she sniffed. 'Especially as the bride and groom are so young. I mean, neither of them's out of university. I can't understand their parents for going along with it. The whole thing will end in tears, you mark my words.'

It was Dad who came to my rescue. Mum said begrudgingly that she'd think about it, but I knew what *that* meant. Dad, on the other hand, said how good it was that Jenna's father had recovered from his heart attack and that the family had something exciting to look forward to. I had to go, he said. It'd be a real experience.

'It's not often that one gets the chance to be a part of something like this. A marriage on New Year's Eve in the frozen northlands on the edge of the Arctic Circle – I'd go if I had the chance,' he said.

And that was that really. Whether there were arguments behind the scenes, I didn't know. Certainly I never heard them. Dad said the trip would have to be my Christmas present, and I said that was fine by me.

But it wasn't fine with Kate. She was furious because, she said, I'd mucked around all term and didn't deserve it. I can't say I blame her. She'd worked all term, but *I* was the one who was going off on the 'great cultural experience', as Dad insisted on calling it.

I felt guilty – but not enough to spoil my excitement. I was flattered to be counted as Jenna's best friend and would have gone to her brother's wedding if it had taken place on an offshore oilrig in the North Sea. Even if it had taken place at home on Carningli Common I'd have gone willingly, and been proud to be invited. But that it was happening somewhere as distant and unknown as Finland was an extraordinary bonus.

Apart from anything else, field trips were the hot subject at school just now. Letters had come home about our Physics trip to the National Centre for Alternative Technology and our French trip to Paris. Our English teacher wanted to take us to Shrewsbury to see the grave of the war poet Wilfred Owen and our Biology teacher wanted to combine it with a visit to the museum there, to find out about Charles Darwin.

Now my Mrs Marridge Project would have a field trip as well. One that mightn't earn me a stupid, useless GCSE, but might actually make a difference to my life. My excitement was heightened by Dad letting loose the fact that he and Mum had met at a wedding. Now I wondered if the same would happen to me. I'd no idea what men were like in Finland, but guessed that they were as capable of falling in love across a crowded church as anybody else.

To this end, I adjusted my Mrs Marridge timetable to accommodate finding my Mr Right – or *se oikea*, as they say in Finland – earlier than expected. Then I got on the Internet and started researching Finnish people and their way of life. My ignorance was total. I knew that we'd be travelling several hundred miles north of Helsinki, but didn't know if people in those frozen northlands lived in ordinary houses or igloos, bought from the supermarket or caught fish on hooks dropped through the ice, travelled in cars or on sleighs pulled by reindeer.

One thing I was certain about, however, was that they'd all be fantastic-looking. I'd never met Marika, but I had seen a photograph of her and she was really beautiful. I reckoned that her sisters, cousins and Finnish girlfriends would be beautiful too. I definitely had to look my best, otherwise no boy would give me a second glance.

But how to look one's best at temperatures of up to minus twenty-five degrees?

Jenna's mother came to my rescue, assuring me that Finns lived ordinary lives in ordinary houses just like everybody else, and I wouldn't need to wrap myself up in reindeer skins in order to stay warm. Finland might be cold in the winter, she said, but its buildings were insulated in a way that made our draughty Welsh houses a bit of a joke. I could wear anything I wanted for the wedding, as long as I dressed carefully when I went outside.

This made things a bit easier when Mum and I went shopping. We couldn't find a dress I liked in Fishguard, so we went to Cardiff instead. I came home in a state of high excitement, unable to believe that I'd been allowed to buy anything so sophisticated. I hung it on the wardrobe door where I could see it day and night – a long red velvet dress lined with silk that made me feel as if I'd achieved 'Woman of Maturity' status at long last.

Dad raised an eyebrow when he saw it and said his little girl was growing up. Mum laughed and said he'd got to face it some time. She gave him a hug and they smiled at each other. I couldn't understand why they were looking at each other like that. Parents can be a mystery sometimes. You never quite know what they're thinking.

After that, the lead-up to the wedding passed in a daze. Everybody else at school was caught up in carol services and Christmas parties, but I was caught up in my field trip. With some help from Jenna, I researched everything I could about Rhys and Marika, starting with their family trees and ending with what their impressions had been when they'd first met.

This was something I wanted to know anyway, for when I met a husband of my own. But I wanted to know it too because of Mum and Dad. What had Rhys and Marika seen in each other that Mum and Dad had failed to find? And what made some couples marry and others live together instead?

I never did find out. Instead I added the question to all the others I hoped to write essays about when I had the time, and returned to the task of researching

Finland. I hadn't even known where it was until I logged on to a map of Europe and saw how close it was to Russia, right on the edge of a huge landmass that extended north-eastwards towards Turkestan, Mongolia and even China.

According to Jenna's father, it was possible to get on a train in the Finnish capital, Helsinki, and travel right over the top of the world, ending up in the Chinese capital, Beijing. The thought of travelling across such a vast wilderness stirred me in ways I could scarcely explain. And Finland stirred me too. It seemed remote and northern and exotic – a vast, lonely land of snow, forests and endless lakes, with a population no bigger than ours in Wales.

I started collecting Finnish phrases, courtesy of the Internet, and Jenna's dad, who was the linguist in the family. *Hyvää yötä* meant 'goodnight', *moi* meant 'hello', but *moi moi* meant 'goodbye', *hei mitä kuuluu* meant 'hi – how are you?' and *kiitos* meant 'thank you'. *Kahvi kiitos* meant 'coffee please'.

Nothing that I learnt was easy to remember, or even remotely recognizable, but Finnish was a noble language, according to Jenna's dad, and it was worth making the effort. It was the language of the Kalevala, which was the oldest recorded folk myth in the world, and it was a shame that so few people could read it, except in translation. This was because, as well as being noble,

Finnish is also hard to learn, its word-endings having a tendency to grow like Pinocchio's nose until they are completely indecipherable.

This was hardly encouraging to somebody like me, who'd never been much good at languages. Nor was it encouraging when Jenna's dad said that the art of speaking Finnish lay in its vowels, which, if pronounced wrongly, could make as grave an error as to turn 'cats' into 'Olympic games'.

In the end, I gave up on Finnish and decided that I'd have to rely on my looks to speak for me. This was none too reassuring, but at least I had my dress to help. When everybody else was asleep at night, I'd put it on, do my hair and make-up, and pace about my bedroom trying to be beautiful by feeling beautiful inside – a tip I'd read about in one of Kate's magazines.

I'd also try to look mysterious by sitting in front of the mirror with a cigarette hanging out of my mouth, saying I wasn't really smoking if I didn't inhale, and I worked on my tolerance to alcohol by nicking wine from the basement, where Dad kept it on tap. Finland, I had discovered, was a land of hardened drinkers, and it was important that I could hold my own. No way did I want to make a fool of myself again by getting drunk the way I'd done at Rebecca's party!

It took for ever to reach the end of term, but finally I got there. I remember sitting on the bus, clutching the Christmas presents that I'd bought for my friends, dimly aware of Jody going on about the wedding. She was trying to make up with me, saying she didn't mind about not going because she understood that Jenna had had to make a difficult choice.

Her attitude was a far cry from Rebecca's. She sat at the back of the bus and refused to look at me. In fact, for the first time ever, she didn't even give me a Christmas present. Not that I cared. In fourteen days from now, I told myself, Rhys and Marika's wedding would be about to take place, and my *se oikea* would be on his way to the church, ready for the moment when our eyes would meet.

Then who knew what would happen? Maybe I'd never come back to Wales. Maybe the wedding laws were different in Finland, and I'd marry at fourteen without parental consent, and stay for ever. There was a chance that Rebecca would never see me again – and then she'd be sorry for not being nicer.

By the time that I got home from school, I couldn't have felt more excited if I'd been a polar explorer leaving base camp. Here at last was what Ms Lloyd-Roberts had once so memorably called 'my opportunity to scale slopes as high as any Everest' and failure simply wasn't an option. The days flew by. Christmas came and went. The evening before my departure, I went for a farewell drink with Jody at the pub. We'd never been to the pub on our own together before, but I felt as if I could do anything that night.

At least, I did until I attempted to buy a pint at the bar and was refused because I didn't have ID. Immediately, this plunged me into a crisis of self-doubt. For weeks now I'd been working on myself, but where had it got me?

I went into the toilet and stared at the mirror. The face that stared back couldn't have looked more miserable. For all the effort I'd put in, I still looked like a little schoolgirl.

'Somewhere in the frozen northlands at the top of the world,' I thought, 'there's a boy waiting for a girl like me. But what's he going to think if his *se oikea* isn't even old enough to buy him a pint?'

11

Se Oikea

At six-thirty in the morning, with not a hint of sunrise in sight, Mum drove me over the Preseli Hills. The headlights of our car pierced the darkness as we left our little corner of Wales on the edge of the ocean and headed out into the wide world. There wasn't another headlight on those silent hills, and I wondered where Jenna's family were, and how far they'd got on their journey.

All the way to the airport, I thought about weddings drawing people together. Right across Wales, and in the wide world beyond, people were heading for that one small church in Finland. In my imagination, I could see them clustering around airport check-ins in far-flung places, with Finnish destinations attached to their luggage and their minds filled up with snow and ice.

When Mum and I reached the airport, however, we were the first to arrive. In our anxiety not to be late, we were even too early to check in. We sat in the entrance hall, waiting for the rest of the party to turn up, drinking coffee and trying to think of things to talk about. Mum had insisted on driving me herself, rather than letting Jenna's family bring me, because she wanted to see me off in person. She kept on checking that I had my passport and ticket, anxious on my behalf because I'd never flown before.

Not that I was anxious. Or so I told myself. My stomach was only churning because I hadn't eaten breakfast – that was all!

When Jenna's family arrived, it gave me something else to think about other than engine failure, wings dropping off and terrorist bombs. They came surging down the check-in hall in a tidal wave of suitcases and hand luggage, hat boxes, snow boots, skis, ice skates, fur coats and even a couple of guitars. Jenna's mum was in charge, and Jenna's dad – as befitted a man who'd only recently recovered from a heart scare – sauntered along behind her, looking determined to take things easy.

When they saw us, there were lots of hugs and kisses. We all checked in together, then Jenna's mum led us off to the restaurant area, where she ordered breakfast all round while waiting for the rest of our party to turn up. I tucked in heartily, determined to enjoy myself despite my funny tummy.

Other members of Jenna's family started arriving, and soon there was a whole crowd of us. I should have remembered everybody's name, as I'd learnt them all on the family tree, but the only ones that stuck in my mind were Jenna's Aunty Cassidy – bright red hair and dressed in black from head to toe – tiny, birdlike Mrs Brophy – her great-grandma on her mother's side – and Caitlin, Jenna's cousin on her father's side, whose name stuck in my mind because she was so pretty – damn her stupid face!

I remembered Simon's name too – he was Rhys's best man – and his brother Greg. I'd watched them walking across the check-in hall, never imagining for a minute that they were anything to do with us. But when they joined our party, my heart did Olympic-standard somersaults.

Simon was pretty good-looking, but much older than me and out of my league. His baby brother Greg, however, could only have been a couple of years older than me, and had the added attraction of being a god. His looks weren't loud or showy, but Brad Pitt had nothing on him, and neither did the boys in my favourite band, the Seven Inches.

Jenna's mum introduced us, and I found myself struck dumb. When you have Greg's attention, he has this way of smiling with his eyes, his head tilting towards you as if no one else matters. His beautiful mouth curls ever so slightly, as if you're sharing some private joke, and you get the feeling that there are only the two of you in the world.

As smiles go, Greg's is a killer. After being blasted with it, I could scarcely get out the word 'hello'. Greg was the hottest thing around — no doubt about it. Jenna introduced him to Mum, and I waited to see her struck dumb too. But she said, 'Nice to meet you,' as if Greg was just some ordinary boy, and launched into a jolly conversation about Christmas trees and skiing, while I stood about feeling like an idiot because I couldn't think of how to join in.

Finally, she noticed that time was getting on, and decided she ought to be heading home. 'Be good,' she said to me, as if such a thing was possible in present company. 'And have a great time. Text me when you get there, if your mobile works.'

Then she disappeared down the escalator without even turning once to look at me or to wave. I knew that she was probably crying. She's hopeless at farewells. Poor old Mum — I certainly wasn't crying, believe me! It took no time at all for me to forget her completely.

Jenna's mother gathered us all together and we made our way through airport security, where, to our amusement, the only one to be searched for guns or drugs was little Mrs Brophy. Then Jenna and I hit the duty-free shops, buying chocolates and magazines for the journey, drooling over the expensive clothes and jewellery and keeping an eye out for Greg. Well, I did — I can't speak for Jenna.

Se Oikea

From the moment I met him, I knew he was my *se oikea*. Even my funny tummy knew it, and stopped rumbling and grumbling as if it realized that, from now on, everything was going to be all right. I mean, what could possibly go wrong with Greg around? I couldn't have felt safer if he'd been James Bond. Even if our plane *did* start going down, I somehow knew he'd turn things round. And if he didn't, what sweeter way to go than by his side?

I *did* have the slightest twinge of nerves when our flight was called. But by the time I'd found my place – with Greg seated right in front of me – calmness had returned. It was destiny that had seated us so close to each other. It was written in the stars. Only last night, I'd read my horoscope in the paper and, on the subject of love, it had said, 'Look forward, not back.'

I settled into my seat, with Greg almost close enough to touch, thinking that there was nowhere on this plane – or anywhere else, for that matter – that I'd rather be. Jenna sat next to me, and Caitlin next to her. She'd got her eyes fixed on Greg too, but I knew I had nothing to worry about – not with the destiny that *I'd* got written in the stars!

The three of us chattered to each other and shared chocolates and magazines. Everything was fine until the plane started taxiing down the runway. Then Caitlin paled, closed her eyes and confessed that she had a fear of flying.

'I wish I hadn't eaten those chocolates,' she said. 'Now I'll probably sick them up.'

Jenna took her hand. In the past, she'd always said she liked flying but now she confessed to never having cared for the taking-off bit. I, on the other hand, loved it! From the moment the plane started gathering speed, my body pressed back against the seat, I loved everything that happened. Until you've tried a thing, you never know how it's going to be.

For me, the very best moment was when I realized we were off the ground. I loved the feeling of being lifted up and up – of my life suddenly being out of my control as something big and powerful took me over. I also loved the way that, when we rose through the clouds, we found the sky blue above them, and the sun shining.

'For the rest of my life,' I thought, 'whenever the sky's grey, I'll remember that the blue's still there above the clouds, and the sun's still shining.'

It was a perfect day. Perfect, but short-lived – for we were flying into the darkness of a northern midwinter, where the sun's appearances were fleeting and the nights were long.

With Greg in front of me, the journey could have lasted for ever, as far as I was concerned. But in no time at all we reached Copenhagen in Denmark, and there were hours to kill before our connecting flight. We explored more duty-free shops and drank endless coffees while we waited for our luggage to be transferred onto the Finnish Helsinki-bound plane.

Finally we set off again, putting our watches forward to comply with Helsinki time. I had the window seat but, this time, there was no sign of Greg. This was a disappointment, but at least it freed me to concentrate on the view.

It was so spectacular that no man — no matter how beautiful — could ever be expected to compete with it. The sun was setting over the rim of the world, and the sky was a mass of gold, black and purple, as if some artist had gone crazy and thrown paint everywhere. Lakes and forests glinted in the sun's last dazzling beams, then the richest, most astonishing darkness fell and the snowy landscape turned a sizzling electric blue. Roads and towns stood out from it like diamonds of light set in deepest velvet night.

But they were few and far between. Mostly we found ourselves flying over a vast wilderness that made Carningli Common and the Preseli Hills seem like tiny places. There were huge forests down there, and frozen lakes and snowy wastelands so large that they looked like snow-bound, frozen seas.

When we reached Helsinki, it was snowing heavily. We had to circle the city twice before being allowed to land. Caitlin was convinced that something was wrong with the plane, but, despite her predictions, it finally descended with all the dignity of a red kite over Cardigan Bay, touching down with only the gentlest of thuds.

As soon as the seat-belt lights went off, Jenna's mother jumped to her feet and started pulling on her fur coat, bought especially for the snow last time she'd been to Finland. She pulled on a thick hat, woolly scarf, extra socks and thermal gloves, laced up her snow boots, did her coat up to her neck and turned up the collar. I thought she was going completely over the top and that a bit of snow never hurt anyone. But, when I stepped off the plane, I realized what she'd been preparing for.

Finland was cold – to put it mildly. Even the few steps to the waiting airport bus were a bracing experience. Breathing in hurt, and breathing out hurt too. The freezing air took my breath away and it was a relief to get to the warmth of the airport terminal. But we still had another flight to make, taking us further north into a region which was going to be even colder.

As the only Finnish linguist among us – though *linguist*, he insisted, was the wrong word – Jenna's dad steered us through the airport and on to our final flight. This time we were on a smaller plane. I slept and woke and slept again. The last leg of the journey was by bus, but I hardly remember getting onto it, let alone leaving the plane, I was that tired.

All I remember is Jenna sitting next to me, and Greg across the aisle from us, Caitlin sitting next to him, purring quietly with contentment. Her eyes were closed, she was breathing gently, as if she was asleep, and her head was sliding slowly down towards his shoulder. I didn't, for a minute, believe that she was really asleep, and neither did Jenna when we talked about it later, over supper.

After that bus journey, I watched Caitlin's every move. She only had to look Greg's way and I was on her case. This was made easier by the fact that we found ourselves sharing a bedroom when we reached the hotel. It was a beautiful old building, set on a hill that overlooked the rest of the town, decorated with painted shutters, arched windows and intricately carved bargeboards. We were on the top floor, the two of us together, with Jenna next door.

It was four flights up to our floor, so Jenna and I took the lift. Caitlin, on the other hand, went up the stairs – *with Greg to help her*. Talk about not missing a trick! She insisted afterwards that she hadn't known there was a lift and certainly hadn't expected anyone to help drag her luggage up all those stairs.

That night, despite my irritation with my room-mate, I slept like a log. Our room was as warm as Jenna's mum had assured me Finnish houses would be. Despite the fact that thick snow lay across everything from the balcony to the forest-bound lake on the edge of town, I needed only the lightest of bedcovers.

In my sleep, I dreamt about that lake. I was skating round it like an Olympic champion, cheered on by everybody in our party, all marvelling at how good I was. The whole town had turned out to watch, from the skiers in the forest to the men who manned the food kiosks set up on the ice. I could smell their meaty Finnish *grillis*, and smell the snow as well. Spotlights were trained on me, and I could see people watching from their windows, and on their balconies and all the way round the harbour, where boats were frozen in the ice.

And Greg was watching too. He smiled that smile of his, for me alone, and I could have skated for ever beneath his gaze.

But it was only a dream. I awoke to find snow on my balcony and remembered where I was. For a split second I almost felt disappointed, but then I jumped out of bed and pulled on my dressing gown. Caitlin was still asleep, which was fine by me. I tiptoed into the bathroom, washed myself, put on my make-up, did my hair and changed my clothes three times before I was convinced that I'd got it right. Then I went downstairs for breakfast, leaving Caitlin to lie in.

Greg was in the dining room already, as I'd hoped he'd be. But so was his brother, Simon, and a party of college friends who'd arrived in the night – and he was far more interested in them than me. Rhys and Marika had arrived as well, having driven over from her parents' house to greet their guests. There was only one day left before the wedding and you could see how excited they were. According to Mum, they should have been crippled by last-minute doubts by now, as the enormity of what they were doing finally sank in. But they looked perfectly happy to me.

We all sat together at one long dining table, making plans for the day. Rhys and Marika had a wedding rehearsal to attend – and so did Simon and the ushers, who included Greg, and Jenna and her parents. The rest of us were free to ski, shop, skate, walk around the lake, visit the local tourist attractions or do anything else we fancied.

But what could I possibly fancy unless it included Greg? I hung around until he'd gone, hoping he'd invite me to go too, but he didn't even look my way. My only comfort was that, by the time Caitlin came downstairs, he was out of her clutches, at least for now.

You could see how cross she was that she hadn't got up earlier, but there was nothing she could do about it. We passed each other in the dining-room doorway. 'You could have woken me,' she said. 'Breakfast's almost finished.'

'I didn't want to disturb you. You looked so peaceful,' I said.

After breakfast, Caitlin went shopping and I tagged along. She tried to shake me off but no way was I letting her out of my sight, just in case she tracked down Greg. We both bought thermal gloves and socks because the ones we'd brought from home were hopelessly inadequate. Then, equipped to face the elements, we explored the town, visiting the ski slopes and the local museum, trailing in and out of shops, navigating icy pavements and walking round the lake, looking northwards towards the Arctic Circle, wondering how far away it was.

We stayed out for hours, despite the cold. It was a different coldness here to the one at home. Drier, and it didn't sink into our bones.

Every now and then we bumped into groups of people from the wedding party, out exploring the town's fine old clapboard houses, its snow-bound parks and wide streets lined with snow-laden trees. It was a beautiful town. I told myself I'd never forget it, and that I'd never forget the quality of daylight either, which was bright and gentle all at the same time – clear and fresh and in ways I can't explain, completely different to the light back home.

But it was quickly come and quickly gone. In no time at all – just as you'd expect in a northern landscape in midwinter – the sun disappeared and darkness rose in its place. We went back to the hotel for a tea of sherry and Finnish cakes, and to meet up with Jenna. Then, in the evening, the wedding party hit the bars.

Everybody came out, first in little groups to eat Mexican together, or meals of reindeer meat served with forest berries, or traditional Russian or Finnish *grillis* off a stall. Then gradually the groups started coming together until finally they all ended up in Marika's brother's favourite Irish theme bar, down by the lake.

He was there already, waiting for us with Rhys, Marika and the wedding party, which included Simon, the best man, and a crowd of Norwegian relatives who'd travelled night and day, over mountains and across fjords, to be here for the wedding. They were obviously determined to enjoy themselves, and so were friends of Rhys's who'd flown in from Hong Kong, and Marika's cousins who'd come all the way from Tokyo!

What a United Nations of a wedding party we were, downing Finnish beer, Mexican tequila, Russian vodka and Irish stout, drawn together by a celebration that meant the same in every country right around the world! Half of us couldn't understand the other half, but it really didn't matter. We communicated anyway. I remembered what Dad had said about this wedding being an experience and knew already that he was right.

More and more people kept turning up, and the

buzz of voices grew all the time. Mrs Brophy broke the rule of her old age by giving herself permission to stay up after her bedtime of nine-thirty. I bought alcohol at the bar and I must have looked old enough because nobody asked for ID. Jenna's parents saw me doing it and didn't say I shouldn't. It was as if we'd all been set free. As if there were no rules any more.

Then Greg came in and everything suddenly lifted on to a whole new plane. I don't know how else to explain it. The Finnish and Norwegian boys were all good-looking, but they didn't stand a chance. Greg was my *se oikea* and no one else would do. I watched him drinking with the Finns, keeping up with them shot for shot, shaking hands, slapping shoulders, finding countless ways to compensate for his inability to speak their language. I had never seen anybody so at home in his own body. There was a grace about him – a confidence that made me unable to take my eyes off him.

Caitlin was just the same. We were like a pair of hawks guarding our prey. Not that Greg even glanced our way. Only when a group of Marika's Finnish cousins joined us did he finally break away from the group that he was sitting with and come over. Perhaps he wanted to warn those boys off, as if we British girls were his territory, or perhaps he wanted to make friends with them. Either way, he obviously didn't want to make friends with *me*. He talked to Jenna, talked to Caitlin – but still didn't glance my way!

In the end, I simply couldn't stand it. Ever since my moment of epiphany halfway through Lucy Chan's funeral, I'd been waiting for Greg. I didn't need any star charts to tell me that. He was the one I'd done my research for, and all that training in maturity. The one I'd known I'd meet across a crowded room and then my life would be changed for ever.

But Greg didn't want me. He didn't feel the same. He was too busy eyeing up everybody else to even notice me. I told myself that this was my chance to put my research into practice, but I knew it wouldn't work. Gods like Greg didn't have the time for girls like me, and if I thought otherwise I was a fool!

I slipped outside, pretending that I was going to the loo. The night was shockingly cold but I didn't care. I stood looking at the lake, feeling overwhelmingly sorry for myself. I knew I couldn't go back inside and decided to return to the hotel.

'Are you all right?' a voice said.

I turned around – and there, to my astonishment, was the man himself, his words coming out in clouds of freezing white breath. I blushed and didn't know what to say. Greg came and stood beside me and looked at the lake too. He was close enough to touch, and I couldn't understand what he was doing here. It almost looked as if he'd followed me outside.

My head starting spinning and I found myself shivering. I swear it wasn't because of the cold – or the alcohol I'd been drinking, but maybe Greg thought it was because he smiled that special smile of his and put an arm around my waist, as if to steady me. Then, without further warning – as if he knew exactly what I wanted, and he wanted it too – he pulled me towards him and *started kissing me*.

It was he who made the first move. It wasn't me, honestly – I mean, I wouldn't have dared. But suddenly his mouth was so hot that it came as a shock, and I had a whole new reason for shivering. Even when he wrapped his coat round me, I couldn't stop. We were burning up together, but I didn't care. Flames licked our faces and ice formed in our hair and if we'd died like that, fused into a single block, I still wouldn't have cared. I mean, *what a way to go!*

Only when a door banged shut and a couple of old Finnish men stepped out into the night did we stop. They stamped past us through the snow, smiling to themselves as if they knew they'd saved us from death by sex. Greg let go of me, buttoned up his coat and turned up his collar.

'People will be wondering where we are,' he said, the words coming out of him unsteadily, as if the cold had really got to him – either that or he'd drunk too much as well.

We returned inside. I couldn't wait for Caitlin to notice us together. Greg headed for a fresh drink and I headed for the stove at the far end of the bar. Standing warming my hands in front of it, I felt as high as any Everest. When Greg didn't come back to me after he'd bought his drink, I didn't mind. I knew that something of major significance had happened between us and nothing in our lives would ever be the same.

Or so I thought for a blissful half-hour – until Caitlin went outside, like I had done, and was gone for ages, and came back looking like the cat who'd got the cream. I looked around for Greg and saw him coming in as well, and that was the moment when I realized that I wasn't special. I was just another girl. Just another conquest. Just a number, that was all. Nothing of significance had happened between us and I had been a fool for thinking otherwise.

I stood there, my stomach churning, feeling sick inside. Marika's brother was talking to me but I couldn't take in a single word he said. If I remember rightly, I may even have walked away from him.

After that, nothing I remember makes much sense. People came and went – including Greg, who never looked at me again, and my only comfort was that he didn't look at Caitlin either. I remember searching for Jenna, wanting to pour out all my troubles, but suddenly she, too, was nowhere to be seen. *Jenna, my best friend Jenna*. She'd been here only a minute ago, but now she'd disappeared, and Greg lay behind it. I knew he did – and how he'd managed to pull the three of us in full view of each other, I never quite worked out.

Later on, staggering back to the hotel along frozen pavements, we started laughing. Caitlin, to her credit, was the one who set us off, shaking her head in disbelief and owning up to making a complete fool of herself. Then Jenna laughed as well, and I ended up laughing too, even though my heart was broken and I'd thought I'd never smile again.

'He's *so* up himself,' Jenna said.

'Did you see him with that Norwegian girl?' Caitlin said.

'If I never saw him again, it'd be too soon,' I said.

We all agreed – which, as we'd have to face Greg at tomorrow's wedding, was a bit unfortunate. It took us a while to get back to the hotel. Caitlin lost her grip and landed face down in the snow, Jenna brought up an evening's worth of alcohol not to say anything of her supper, and I cursed my wasted chances with Marika's brother, swearing that I wouldn't do a thing like that again.

12

Royal Superstars

Next morning, I woke up seriously hung-over. In fact, all three of us did. We dragged ourselves down to breakfast feeling pretty sorry for ourselves. Even the fact that Greg was nowhere to be seen didn't improve our mood.

After breakfast, we went out shopping to fill in time before the wedding in the afternoon, buying presents to take home with us. We were a subdued little group, and we kept on bumping into other subdued little groups of wedding party guests who couldn't quite believe how much alcohol they'd put away last night. Even Rhys – who we bumped into with arms full of bouquets – said he had a headache and was relieved that the wedding wasn't until four o'clock.

But he looked so happy that it couldn't help but rub off. He disappeared down the street and our spirits lifted. Suddenly there was more to life than hangovers and sleazy boys. We ate lunch together at a *grilli* bar, taking photographs of each other and promising eternal friendship. Then we returned to the hotel to find that the tables had been decorated with silver horseshoes, tall candles in cut-glass holders and snow-white roses.

A thrill of excitement ran through us like an electric shock. It was time, at last, to get dressed up! In only an hour, the coach would arrive to take us all to the church. We dashed upstairs, too impatient to wait for the lift. As far as I was concerned, the bride counted for nothing, and neither did anybody else. There was only one thing that mattered at this wedding. *My red velvet dress.*

I showered, washed my hair and wriggled my way into the dress, luxuriating in the feel of its silky lining against my skin. Jenna had already said she loved it a hundred times over, but now Caitlin said she loved it too. In a gesture of generosity, she lent me a pair of long black gloves that she said didn't go with her outfit but would look perfect with mine. I thanked her from my heart, hoping she'd never know how much I'd hated her when we'd first met.

Jenna did my hair, and I did hers, and the three of us pooled our make-up and did each other's faces. By the time we descended the stairs, we felt like supermodels on a catwalk. Whether anybody actually noticed us is open to debate. But we felt terrific anyway.

The hotel lobby was crowded, everybody waiting for

the coach. The only person who wasn't ready was Jenna's mum, who came hurtling through in a dressing gown, calling in a voice that bordered on hysteria that her travel iron was broken and did anyone have a spare?

In the end, however, even she was ready, and the coach set off. It was the first time since arriving in the dark that we'd seen anything of the countryside beyond the city's limits and we were full of curiosity. The coach took us round the lake, passing huge, illuminated ski jumps and a forest full of floodlit ski paths, then it cut off across open country. It was only three-thirty in the afternoon, but already the sun was going down. In the twilight, the moon and stars were starting to light up and the landscape beneath them sparkled like sequinned silk.

At one point, the coach stopped to let a herd of reindeer cross the road. At another, we raced a train until it drew ahead of us and faded into the night. Was it travelling the Helsinki to Beijing line? I watched it disappear, imagining myself being whisked away across the wilderness at the top of the world.

But when I caught a first glimpse of the church, I wouldn't have wanted to be anywhere else. We came round a great loop in the road – snowy fields on either side, like a blue sea at night – and the church stood ahead of us, framed by trees. In the sky above it, more stars shone than I had ever seen in my life.

Slowly the coach drew closer until it stopped outside the gatehouse, which looked like the entrance to a fairy castle. We pulled on our coats and piled out into the snow. The gatehouse was floodlit, and so was the path beyond it, which had been swept and gritted for the occasion. The church door was wide open and full of light.

And framed in it stood Greg.

At the sight of him, everything fell flat. All day long, I'd tried to tell myself that he wasn't really that attractive, but in his wedding finery he looked good enough to eat. The three of us squared up to him.

'*Idiot!*' Jenna muttered under her breath.

'*Bastard!*' Caitlin said.

'*Who does he think he is?*' I said.

Greg saw us coming and tried on his smile. But we swept past him into church, our heads held high. We didn't even look his way when he handed us our orders of service. We had better things to look at, things like the interior of the church, for example, which was vaulted and candlelit, decorated with statues and ancient wall paintings. It looked like something out of another world – and so did the groom.

Standing at the front in his wedding suit and white bow tie, Rhys looked like a completely different boy to the one that Jenna and I had spent the night with when their dad was rushed to hospital. I followed

Caitlin into the pew and sat down wondering why it had never occurred to me to fancy him before. He looked even better than Simon, who was standing next to him, fiddling with his cuffs and straightening his buttonhole.

But then all the men looked pretty sensational. I looked around, and maybe it was a trick of the candle-light but it seemed to me that the church was packed full of male beauty of the highest order. Even Jenna's dad looked good – in an old-mannish sort of way. And, as for all the Finnish and Norwegian boys – well, words defeat me.

I settled back to feast my eyes. But no sooner had I started enjoying myself than the organ thundered and the congregation rose to its feet. Suddenly nothing else counted, because the bride was in the church. For a moment, she stood framed in the huge old church door, then she started up the aisle on her father's arm.

The moment was theirs alone. Marika looked stunning, and her father was bursting with pride. Everybody sighed. Caitlin squeezed my hand and I squeezed hers, and Jenna's eyes started watering and so did mine. For the rest of the service, I swear we never gave another thought to Greg. Even when he slipped into the pew next to us, his tasks over for now, we didn't give him a thought.

Our eyes were on Rhys, making his vows in English, and Marika, making hers in Finnish, and on the priest, standing before them in a gown of white and gold, incanting prayers that turned them into man and wife.

Afterwards the wedding guests lined the church path, as is the custom at Finnish weddings, waiting for the bride and groom to emerge. That's the moment I'll always remember. They came out of that church like royal superstars, and the Finnish guests threw rice and the English ones confetti, and camera flashlights popped everywhere and video cameras rolled. Marika's long dress swept behind her like a queen's train. The bell in the gatehouse tower rang out across the snowy landscape and Arctic foxes barked in the darkness, as if even they had been caught up in the moment.

Back at the hotel, we rocked and rolled, and ate and drank, and laughed and made speeches for the rest of the night. All sorts of funny little things stick out in my mind, like Jenna's Aunty Cassidy in pink instead of black, and Mrs Brophy dancing with Marika's father, while Jenna's father threw caution to the winds and jived vigorously with a beautiful blonde Finnish girl with dreadlocked hair.

On the plane out to Helsinki, somebody had told Jenna that Finnish weddings were unforgettable. Now we knew what they'd been on about. The evening was full of surprises – Marika's kidnapping, for example, when custom had it that Rhys had to pay a string of forfeits to win her back. And the way the two of them had to stand on chairs to kiss every time the wedding guests demanded it by banging spoons on the table.

Then there was the wedding waltz – Rhys and Marika whirling round the room while Marika's little cousins, dressed in traditional costumes, chased after them blowing bubbles. And there were party games too – every forfeit taking the form of a gift of a good turn for the bride and groom.

And then, at midnight, there were the fireworks.

I had forgotten that it was New Year's Eve, and had no idea, anyway, how Finns went about celebrating it. But on the first stroke of midnight, the sky was suddenly full of light. It stretched right across the town as if, just for that one moment, the darkness of the northern night could be driven away.

We went outside to watch, standing in the hotel garden and looking into the sky. The town clock struck twelve times and everybody wished everybody else *hyvää uutta vuotta*, as they say in Finland, and *godt nytt år*, as they say in Norway, *blwyddyn newydd dda* as they say at home in Wales, *wan an* as they say in Hong Kong, and *oyasuminasai* as they say in Tokyo. We mightn't have been able to speak each other's languages, but there were things that went beyond words, and this moment together was one of them.

After the fireworks, we returned inside to dance until the bride and groom departed for their secret wedding-night destination. Then the party began to draw to a close. A last few determined drinkers sat toasting each other, celebrating the fact that 'we're all family now'. Greg had long since disappeared and I wondered which lucky girl had the pleasure of his company this time.

Caitlin set off for our room, with Jenna trailing behind her, looking happy but exhausted. The lift was out of order and the thought of staggering up four flights of stairs didn't appeal to me, so I sneaked back into the lounge instead, pulled a couple of armchairs together and fell asleep on them.

The last thing I remember seeing was snow falling outside the window, and the last thing I remember thinking was that I ought to make some notes for my Mrs Marridge Project, while the memories were still fresh.

As if I'd ever forget!

Nick
Nick
Nick
Nick
Nick
Nick

I ❤ U

Part V
The Mocks

* *
* *
* *
* *
* *

Nick

Nick Nickk Nickk Nickkkk
Nick
Nick

'NICK'

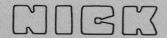

NIC
NICK
KKKK
NICK
NICK
NICK

NICK

NICK

13

Eagle's Eyrie

Next morning, I woke up crying. At first I couldn't work out why, because I wasn't miserable and it didn't make sense. Then I thought that I was crying with happiness for Rhys and Marika. But then it dawned on me that I was crying because something had changed, thanks to the wedding. *I* had changed. I'd woken up with a whole new insight into marriage.

Suddenly I knew it wasn't something I could plan for, like a GCSE exam. There were things that couldn't be fixed with lists and charts and coursework essays, and marriage, I realized, was one of them. You couldn't make it happen just by cutting out articles from news-papers and analysing data. It simply didn't work like that. You could spend the rest of your life collecting case studies and compiling questionnaires, but there'd always be something missing because you couldn't pin down love, or measure it or make it happen just to order.

And, without love, marriage didn't stand a chance.

For that entire day, I felt as if the bottom had dropped out of my world. A cross-country skiing party along forest paths failed to raise my spirits, and so did the evening flight home. In fact it was a horrible journey, passing over frozen northlands until they felt like a distant fantasy – not unlike my marriage project, I thought to myself.

Everybody else was half asleep, bathing in the wedding's afterglow, but I sat wide awake, trying to write down how I felt and at least redeem something from the tatters of my field trip. But I wasn't in the mood, and I couldn't find the words, and what was the point anyway if I wasn't going to get a marriage out of it?

To make matters worse, I returned home to find Kate's mock exams about to start, which meant that the atmosphere in our house – which had been so relaxed over Christmas – had suddenly become supercharged. You'd have thought she was sitting the real thing. She looked as if she'd shatter if you even breathed on her, and Mum and Dad were behaving as if nothing else mattered apart from her well-being.

At school too the attitude was scarcely less tense. A seclusion zone had been thrown around the exam room, with notices up in every corridor in a ten-mile radius warning that anyone who as much as raised their voices above the level of a whisper while the mocks were taking place would face a week's worth of detentions.

You'd have thought the exam room was an execution chamber. Every now and then, glimpses of examinees would be caught as they shuffled in, and you'd get a tingle of excitement as if catching sight of condemned women. It was as bad as that. I'm honestly not exaggerating.

In addition, I had some tests of my own coming up, and was totally unprepared. By the time I'd been home a couple of days, it almost felt as if the wedding had never happened. Everybody around me had put Christmas behind them and was getting on with their work, including Jenna.

I knew I was meant to do the same but, for all my trying, I couldn't concentrate. I'd sit at my desk and pretend to look interested, but if my teachers had known about the total void inside my head, they'd have whisked me straight off to the nearest educational psychologist!

The work was really piling up as well. Every day, the importance of doing this for my future was drummed into me. And every night, I was sent home with fresh mountains of homework. The only crumb of comfort came from the fact that the whole class was being given the same treatment. We'd get together on the bus home and complain bitterly about the stress we were under. You'd have thought that all the adults in our lives had entered into a conspiracy to stop us ever being happy or having fun.

The Mocks

We didn't get it. We really didn't. The world was populated with vicious sadists who, if they weren't teachers, all happened to be parents. And mine were the worst, I swore they were. Mum was a particularly vicious sadist, along the lines of Ms Lloyd-Roberts herself.

And even Dad was one. He'd fought for me to go to Finland and have a good time, but now you'd think the immortal words *good time* had never passed his lips. Good times were out and hard work was in. Once Mum had been the one who came upstairs to check on me, but now Dad did too. It was as if she'd passed on to him some sort of vile nagging disease, or he'd had a sense-of-humour bypass operation.

'It's not what you *dream* about, it's what you *do* that counts,' he went on at me one evening when he came upstairs, drawn by my radio, to find me staring blankly into space.

I'd heard that one before. It was one of Dad's favourite sayings, all the more irritating from a man whose almost every evening was spent slumped in front of the telly.

'Life's a barrel of beer, there for the drinking,' I countered with another. 'You've got to seize your chances and drain them deep.'

'Don't you get funny with me!' Dad said, recognizing what I was doing.

'You've got to laugh or else you'll die,' I countered yet again.

Dad flushed. I could have gone on like that for hours and he knew it. Normally he didn't mind being teased – and he certainly did plenty of it himself – but not tonight.

'So, this is how you repay me for letting you go to Finland against your mother's better judgement, is it?' he snapped.

There was no answer to that, apart from feeling mildly ashamed of myself for having let him down. But, in no time at all, I couldn't have cared less. There were so many arguments that week that, by Saturday morning, I was like a time bomb primed to explode. Hardly surprisingly, I got into a fight with Kate. We don't often have them, but when we do we go off like sky rockets.

We were sitting at the breakfast table, arguing about whose turn it was to take the dog for a walk. Mum and Dad had gone out shopping in the Millennium Falcon, leaving instructions for one of us to exercise Lizzie. Kate reckoned she shouldn't have to do it, because of her mocks. You'd have thought nobody but her ever had to do any work.

The argument took off from there. There was no stopping us. Names went flying everywhere and every grudge we'd ever held against each other was dredged up, along with whose success meant more in life, who was loved the most and who was brainiest. In the end, Kate stormed off to her bedroom, saying she'd never eat at the same table as me again.

'See if I care. You hardly eat anything anyway. You've probably got anorexia, and good riddance if you die,' I shouted after her.

Mum came in at that point. She wouldn't listen when I tried to explain that I'd been provoked beyond endurance, but accused me of gross insensitivity. She always took Kate's side. I stormed out of the house, declaring that I wasn't coming back. I don't suppose she believed me. I mean, I'm always saying things like that.

I meant it, though. I'd move down to Grandad's hut, I decided, and live there until he started taking bookings for the summer season. I could get a little job to pay for food and the electricity meter, and it might be damp and miserable down there, but surely I'd learnt something over the months I'd been working on the Mrs Marridge Project and would be able to cook and look after myself. Nobody would miss me at home – or so I tried to tell myself – and I wouldn't miss them either. And I wouldn't go to school, not if I didn't want to. And nobody would ever tell me what to do again.

But dreams are one thing and life's another. It only took the hut itself to make me see that. Unlike the grand Victorian houses down on the seafront, with their plate-glass conservatories, stripped-pine kitchens and central heating, Grandad's hut was dark and squalid. Apart from the big front window – which was usually thick with sea spray – there was precious little view and even less warmth or light. Mould grew on the walls and no matter how much scrubbing I might do, or moving around of furniture, I knew I didn't stand a chance of shaking off the atmosphere of gloom left behind by all those holidaymakers who'd rented the place just once, never to come back.

So I decided to cut my losses and move down to the clapboard house on the estuary instead, where I'd looked through the windows and imagined living another life. I also decided to take the Mrs Marridge Project with me – not because I ever intended to work on it again, but because the damp had found its way into the metal box and half the pages were growing brown spots. I also took some blankets, a couple of plates and cups, a candle and a holder, and some knives and forks, packed tightly into a plastic bucket because it was all that I could find in Grandad's kitchen.

I knew it would be easy for Mum and Dad to track me down to Grandad's hut, but that they'd never find me in my eagle's eyrie on the other side of the estuary. I'd be safe from their nagging, and safe from Kate as well. And it was light up there, perched high above the sea – and light was what I wanted, and space too.

Light to see and space to think.

It took me half the morning to find the place again, but when I did it was exactly as I remembered it. As soon as I saw the verandas, with their view of the estuary, I knew I had made the right decision. I forced my way between bramble bushes, kicked open the front door and walked straight in as if I owned the place. The house was even more run-down than Grandad's hut, but it had an entirely different feel to it.

It was the perfect place to think. No teachers would interrupt me here. No sister would argue with me. No parents would come bursting in, pretending to bring me cups of coffee but actually prying into how I was getting on. I settled myself on one of the window seats and suddenly – completely unexpectedly – all the words I'd wanted to write on the plane came pouring out of me.

There was nothing I could do to stop them. You'd have thought a dam had burst. I grabbed a stack of pages out of the tin box scribbled the heading 'Why Get Married?'and started writing things down. I'd scarcely been able to think about my marriage project since the morning after the wedding, let alone put things into words, but now I couldn't stop.

At school they say that, in order to write a good essay, you've got to follow a clear plan, make sure to put in lots of adjectives, and show you know what metaphors and similes are, by giving examples. Well, that day I produced a piece of writing that was everything a grade-A essay should be in terms of inspiration but didn't include a single word I didn't actually want to say. There wasn't a metaphor in the whole thing, nor were there any adjectives. And I didn't read my work back afterwards, like you're meant to do, to check my spelling and punctuation. I didn't draw up or consult a plan. Didn't redraft anything.

I simply wrote what I wanted, the way I wanted, and meant what I wrote. And, by the time I'd finished, I didn't need a grade to tell me I'd written the best essay of my life. No one but me would ever read it – my English teacher would carry on with her 'Could do better's, never knowing that I already had – but I didn't care.

For a moment I savoured my triumph, thinking that, if the worst came to the worst and my marriage plans fell through, I could always become a writer.

Then I put my essay aside – and decided to clean the house. Restless and exhilarated, I found myself wanting to do something practical and energetic.

Not that I'd ever fancied doing housework before. In fact, the echoing silence on that particular subject in the pages of my marriage project spoke volumes for how I'd always felt about it. But suddenly it no longer seemed like a waste of time. Instead it felt worthwhile and significant.

'Perhaps I want to give something back to the house for giving something to me,' I thought. 'I don't know. Or perhaps this is the Wendy house that Mum never let me have because she thought it was a sexist toy.'

Either way, I went down to the basement, found a scratchy old broom head without a handle, filled Grandad's plastic bucket with cold water from a stream down the bottom of the garden and started work. I brushed the cobwebs off the ceilings, washed the windows inside and out, scrubbed the floors, swept the verandas, aired Grandad's blankets on the bramble bushes in the bright sunshine, collected dead wood from the trees, cleaned out the grate and lay a fire.

It took the rest of the day and, by the time I'd finished, I was completely worn out. But my sense of satisfaction made it all worthwhile. It was nearly night-time by now. In Finland it would have been dark for ages. I wrapped the blankets round me and sat before the unlit fire, not caring that I'd brought no matches, because the fire in my imagination was a hundred times warmer than a real one could be, and a hundred times more beautiful.

Outside, clouds were blowing in from the sea, bringing a storm with them. I could hear wind whistling past the windows and see trees and bushes shaking. I thought about the little Finnish church with its hundreds of candles. Thought about Rhys and

Marika standing at the altar, saying, 'I do.' I was safe because I had my eagle's eyrie, but they were safe because they had each other.

I envied them, I really did. It was lonely being me, living in my secret world. I might have friends and family to look out for me, but no one had a clue about the world inside my head. I had no one to tell it to. For all that my family loved me, and my friends were always there for me, I had no one I could bring myself to trust enough.

I sat in the darkness, knowing that Mum and Dad would be worrying by now and I should be heading back. But I couldn't tear myself away. Everything I'd done today – all the jobs, and everything I'd written, and everything I'd thought about as well – had been one total act of inspiration. But something was still to come. *I knew it was.* I could feel it waiting to reveal itself, almost close enough to touch. If there'd been a knock at the door and it had come striding in, bringing love with it, and yet more inspiration, and everything else I'd ever wanted, I wouldn't have been surprised.

I closed my eyes and waited, but it didn't come that night.

I had to wait until next day.

14

Love

And it happened too. I fell in love, I mean. It happened just like I'd expected. I was walking Lizzie down by the estuary, trying to make up to Mum and Dad for the row we'd had last night, when I got home. Lizzie picked up a big black dog and set off with him as if some pack instinct I didn't even know she possessed had taken over. I went running after her, but at the irresistible whiff of dog odour she refused to respond to my stern commands to 'come here', 'sit' and 'stay'.

In fact, the two dogs were as bad as each other. It definitely wasn't only Lizzie to blame. Not that the owner of the other dog saw it that way! He'd thought he was out on a nice leisurely stroll with his Walkman, but before you could say 'Red Hot Chilli Peppers' he found himself chasing across salt marshes, up and down sand dunes, over cliffs and along beaches, getting soaking wet because of the high tide.

He swore all the way and, running to keep up with him, I bore the brunt of his anger. You'd have thought the whole thing was my fault. We finally found the dogs competing in a sheep-worrying competition, and he exploded with fury, accusing Lizzie of leading his dog astray.

It was ridiculous, of course – I mean, our Lizzie would never lead anyone astray – but it was only when I dropped onto hands and knees and crawled along the edge of the cliff, whispering 'Clever girl!' and 'Well done!' that he saw the funny side of anything.

Even then, he didn't see it at first, but stared at me as if I were mad. But I knew what I was doing. If I'd approached Lizzie in any other way, she'd have charged off across the cliff, chasing some other sheep and putting herself in danger of being popped by a farmer's shotgun.

My strategy worked, as well. Lizzie warmed to my approval and came bounding over, wagging her tail as if to say, 'Aren't I a clever dog?' For a reward I pounced on her, clapped her in chains and dragged her off the cliff, shouting, 'I'm *ashamed* of you.'

That was when the other dog's owner started laughing. We left the cliff, our pets in tow, and he asked if I knew how funny I'd looked crawling along like that, praising my dog for trying to kill a sheep? He also apologized for shouting at me, and told me that his name was Nick. I agreed that I might have looked slightly funny, and told him that my name was Elin, which, for some reason, made us laugh all the more. We couldn't stop either – not until we looked at each other properly for the first time and recognized each other *from Lucy Chan's funeral.*

That certainly shut us up. I dried my eyes.

'We've met before, haven't we?' Nick said. He was the boy who'd shared Mum's tissues – the one I'd thought was Lucy's lover.

'Yes,' I said. 'We have.' And that was the moment when I looked into his eyes and true love struck.

Nick felt it too. I know he did, because the look he gave me swept me clean off my feet. Suddenly this was nothing like what I'd felt in Finland when I thought that Greg was my *se oikea.* I was Nick's fair lady and he was my white knight – and I know exactly what I'm talking about here, because I saw something like it once on the telly. Some schoolgirl's favourite pop star turned up at her school for a game-show prank. He was dressed in armour and riding a white steed, and he swept into her classroom, picked her up in his arms, whisked her out of school and rode off with her. Everybody hung out of the windows to watch it hap-pening – the teachers, the school cleaners, her best friends, her worst enemies, *everybody.*

And this felt even better than that!

We walked along the beach together, talking about Lucy's funeral and how dreadful it had been. Nick hadn't been Lucy's lover but her cousin. His memories of her brought tears to his eyes, and it felt like the most natural thing in the world to put my arm round him.

We walked in silence, and the silence felt completely comfortable. Then, slowly, Nick started telling me about himself – things like which A levels he was taking, and what his hobbies were, and about the work he did part-time in the family takeaway. He had a hard slog ahead of him, he reckoned, but it would be worth it because, by the time that he was thirty, he wanted a whole chain of takeaways of his own.

Nick was nothing if not ambitious. I warmed to his certainties in life. I'd never met anyone, apart from myself, who had such a clear-cut sense of what they wanted to achieve. We were two of a kind. Nick asked about my own ambitions and, sensing that I didn't know him well enough yet to be entirely frank, I said the first thing that came into my head.

'I want to be a writer,' I said.

Nick was impressed. By this time, we'd worked our way back along the beach to his old beat-up car and could simply have apologized for our terrible mutts and gone our separate ways. But he made some thin excuse about the dogs needing more time to dry off and we did the walk again. We couldn't get enough of each other, walking ever slower as if we didn't want our time together to end, talking about books I'd read at school, and plays I'd done, and what I'd liked about them, and how they'd influenced me 'as a writer'.

I was hard pressed to remember anything I'd liked enough to talk about, let alone call an *influence*. But Nick kept asking, and I managed to interest him enough to want to know what I'd written myself.

'What are you working on at the minute?' he said.

'I'm working on a novel set in Finland,' I replied.

'That's a coincidence. My mother's sister's best friend, Cassidy, has just come back from a wedding in Finland,' he said.

We both agreed what a small world it was. By this time, we were back at the car. It seemed like the obvious thing to agree to meet up again. It didn't even feel like a date, just two friends arranging when they'd next be free. When Nick said, 'Perhaps we could go to the cinema, or something,' it felt like the most natural thing in the world to answer, 'Yes,' and when he said, 'How about Wednesday?' to answer, 'That's fine by me. Down at the bus shelter by the crossroads – Here's my mobile number. Phone when you know what time.'

When I got home, I was in a state of shock. So was Mum, when she saw what I'd done to Lizzie. I tried to explain that it was more a matter of what Lizzie had done to me, but she pointed out that I wasn't the one who was covered in mud. I owned up about the sheep and she blanched and said that if I couldn't control

Lizzie – and I obviously couldn't – then someone else would have to walk her.

As the *someone else* in question was likely to be Kate, you can imagine the glares I got from that quarter! I beat a hasty retreat to my bedroom, saying I'd wasted enough time already and had got to get on with some homework.

It was a good excuse and I stayed up there for most of the day. I told myself that I was working, but really I was daydreaming. One thing led to another very easily. Undying passion was just a stone's throw from a first date, and an engagement from undying passion and a wedding on my sixteenth birthday after that. I knew it wasn't possible to compete with Finland in the romantic-wedding stakes, so I dreamt up a castle in Spain instead, or a beach wedding in the Caribbean, or a chapel in Las Vegas, complete with crooning Elvis lookalikes.

That I might just be jumping ahead of myself never once crossed my mind. I clicked with Nick, and Nick clicked with me, and this was true love, *this was it*. How I was going to persuade my parents to hire a castle in Spain, let alone give their permission for me to marry, seemed no more a problem than how I was going to get out of the house for my first date.

This minor problem was solved by Mum and Dad having a date of their own on the night in question, meeting up with friends in Aberystwyth – which meant they had to leave early to drive all the way across Ceredigion, and would be back late. They came to my room to say goodbye, and didn't have a clue that the chaos greeting them had anything to do with an article open on my bed, entitled 'DRESS TO IMPRESS ON YOUR FIRST DATE'.

Kate knew, though. After my triumph on the Lizzie-walking front, she was on my case. At five to seven, sneaking out the door, she caught me in her high-heeled boots and Mum's gold chain, there to 'keep things nice and simple' – according to the article – while 'adding feminine allure'.

'Where d'you think *you're* going?' she said, leaping out of the shadows.

'I'm not going anywhere,' I said – which wasn't the cleverest answer I've ever given.

Kate blocked my path, glaring at her boots.

'If you must know, I'm going round to Jody's,' I said. She didn't move.

'To revise for a test,' I said.

'Oh yes, without your books?' she said. 'Perhaps I'll come down with you, just to check. I might as well. Lizzie needs a walk and *someone's* got to do it.'

She turned to get her jacket, and I was gone, tearing down the road to the bus shelter, and she didn't stand a chance of catching up. I'd always been quicker than Kate and now it stood me in good stead, even in high-heeled boots. I hid in the corner of the shelter, my eyes fixed on the crossroads, waiting for Nick's car to pull up.

When it did, Kate was immediately forgotten. I leapt in beside him and, if I'd harboured any last-minute doubts about this being a proper date, they were dispelled immediately by his leaning across and kissing me. It was the perfect start to what, I just knew, was going to be the perfect date. We drove into Fish-guard, talking all the way. It was as if we both had everything to say and had suddenly found the exact right person to say it to.

Even in the cinema, we couldn't shut up. We talked all the way through the film, unable to stop even when people hissed at us. Afterwards, I didn't have a clue what the film had been about. Nick apologized for taking me to see such a pile of junk but, given that he'd laughed and chattered all the way through, I'd no idea how he knew that it was junk.

We walked through town together, arm in arm. I thought that, even if I was married, I couldn't possibly be happier. Nick bought some beers and takeaway pizza.

'Where shall we go?' he said. 'Any ideas? Anywhere will do, as long as I've got you to myself.'

We could have gone anywhere – the long harbour wall with its great view of the town; Carningli Com-mon; Newport beach; Grandad's hut; *anywhere*. And, if we had, things would have turned out differently. But, in a moment's craziness, I said, 'I know this house . . .' and then there was nothing I could have done to change things. The die was cast.

We drove back along the highway and, on one side of us, the sea was black and, on the other, the moon lit our path. It was a moon for love, full and white. Nick parked his car on the lane above the house and we walked down to it, kissing all the way. I could scarcely believe that this was happening to me. Only a few days ago, I'd sat before a cold fire waiting for my future, and now here it was – walking through the door with its arms wrapped round me!

Not only that but everything was ready, as if I'd prepared it especially. The fire was laid in the grate, waiting to be lit, as was the candle on the mantelpiece. The corners were swept clean, not a cobweb in sight, and blankets were spread out on the floor, ready for us to lounge back drinking beer, eating pizza and exchanging slow, luscious, lingering kisses that bore no remote resemblance to my quick snog in Finland, courtesy of Greg.

Everything was perfect – until the fire went out. Perhaps the sticks were damp or there wasn't enough kindling. We looked round for more, in a hurry to return to the more important matter of kissing. The room shivered in the darkness. I found a handful of leaves in a corner somewhere, missed out when I'd done my cleaning, and Nick found a tin box of newspaper cuttings on a window seat.

'These'll do,' he called. 'God knows how long they've been here, but they're not too damp.'

He'd found my marriage project! He didn't know that, of course, any more than I knew – until that very moment – that I'd left it on the window sill the other day and forgotten to pack it away. He didn't even know there *was* such a thing as a marriage project. But now he tipped it all out into the grate, throwing on some extra pages for good measure – and I didn't need to see the writing on them to know what *they* were!

I stared in horror as Nick took my handful of leaves and piled it on top of *the best essay I'd ever written*! What was I going to do? Either I had to pretend that the essay meant nothing to me, and let Nick burn it along with everything else, or I had to claim the project as my own, in which case he was bound to want to read it. For the first time, I realized what my words '*I know this house . . .*' might cost me.

I looked at Nick. I'd hardly known him any time at all and, for all our endless talking to each other, there were still things about him that I had to find out. But one of them, I guessed, was that he wouldn't get my 'Why Get Married?' essay. If he read it, he'd have a fit. If he read the rest of my project, and discovered the real

me, he'd have a fit. And, as for the Elvis lookalikes —
they didn't bear thinking about!

'Are you all right?' Nick said — but the words were
scarcely out before I flung myself at the fireplace and
started pulling out my essay.

'What are you doing?' Nick said, striking a match.

I dragged out everything else as well.

'Is that stuff yours?' he said.

I said it wasn't, but clutched it tightly. He burst out
laughing and I turned bright red. He took a step
towards me and I backed away. Only minutes ago, I'd
been in his arms, but now I couldn't get far enough
away.

'Of course it's yours,' he said. 'Come on, Elin. What
have you got there? *Show me.*'

As far as he was concerned, the whole thing was a
great joke. He held out his hand, but I clutched my
project to me and insisted I wasn't hiding anything.
There was an edge of desperation to my voice, but
Nick failed to pick up on it.

'Oh, but you *are* hiding something!' he said. 'Of
course you are. Come on. Spit it out. Let's see what it is!'

As he spoke, he lunged towards me. His eyes sparked
with the fun of teasing me. I might hate it, but he was
having a great time.

'Get away!' I cried.

But I was too late. His snatch-and-grab attack had

already resulted in triumph and he was prancing round the room, brandishing a handful of pages.

'Give those back!' I yelled.

But there was no way Nick was going to do anything like that. He took his trophies over to the candle-light and started reading out loud. I tried everything I knew to get them back, but he held them out of reach.

They couldn't have been worse pages, either! '*How to Become a Woman of Maturity – My Top Ten Tips,*' Nick read.

I mean, how bad was that?

'One, *Breasts,*' he went on. 'Two, *Responsibility.* Three, *Style*. Four, *Self-confidence*. Five, *Good sex* – stop hitting me, Elin! Six, *Good clothes*. Seven, *A Good Heart*. Eight, *Toughness* – get your bloody high heels off me, will you! Nine, *A Bank Account*. And Ten, *Something to do with* – God, Elin – give that back!'

Finally I'd succeeded in getting the Top Tips off him. But he still had a pile of other pages, and he carried on reading, darting round the room with the candle, refusing to stop.

'*My Two-year Countdown to the Big Day,*' he read. ' "*Research*", "*Case Studies*", "*Field Work*", "*Coursework Folder*", "*Revision*", "*Mocks*", "*Study Leave*" and "*The Real Thing*" – in other words, the Big Day itself, when nobody will stop me from getting married and achieving my life's ambition. Not Mum and Dad. Not ANYONE.*'

'You've no right!' I wailed. 'Give that to me.'

But the damage was done. Nowadays my Top Tip of them all is to 'Never talk of marriage on a first date', but for then it was too late. Nick's smile went in like the sun before a storm. The joke was over. A coldness crept into his face as he realized what a basket case he was dating. Nothing — not even sexy high-heeled boots — could help me now.

'I can explain the whole thing, if you'll only listen,' I said — then burst into tears, because I knew couldn't.

The date was over from that moment. I'd known the Mrs Marridge Project would freak Nick out, but being right gave me no satisfaction. I wanted him to come and put his arms round me and tell me that it didn't matter — anything I wrote was fine by him. But it didn't happen. Perhaps Nick didn't realize how much I needed it, or perhaps he simply wasn't into lying.

Either way, he plainly didn't want to be there any more, and neither did I. Everything was spoiled and it was all my fault.

I tried to stop crying but only wept all the harder. No one likes a girl who cries on her first date. When I finally dried my eyes, Nick had put the candle back on the mantelpiece and was getting into his coat. My project lay all over the floor, and that was the end of our romance. I tried to smooth things over, but my pathetic attempt to act as if nothing had happened didn't help.

We didn't even go home together. Nick suggested driving me back, but you could see the relief on his face when I said no. He hurried off, convinced that the nice girl he'd met on the beach had been nothing but an illusion, leaving me convinced that true love might exist, but not for me.

'When will I learn?' I thought, crossing the room and picking up my project, sheet by sheet.

I packed it all back in its box and hid it away somewhere deep and safe where nobody would ever find it if they were looking for kindling. Then I walked home very slowly, taking half the night. Mum and Dad were still up when I got in, sitting in front of the telly with glassy eyes, waiting to tell me how much trouble I was in, yet again. Kate came out to smirk as I walked past her bedroom door. She should have been asleep hours ago, but had stayed awake to savour my disgrace.

What a day it had been, starting with love and ending like this! I climbed into bed, lay my head on the pillow and stared at the darkness with eyes that refused to close. I'd thought I'd found the real thing but had got it wrong. It had just been a mock. Just another practice run – and my grade was F for failure, yet again.

15

Wild Swans

Next morning I didn't go to school. I couldn't face it, especially as I had a test first thing on pre-1914 love poetry, and love was definitely something that I didn't want to think about. I tore up my stupid Mrs Marridge timetable and threw it in the bin, along with my motto, 'Application is the Key', and my English coursework sheets on Andrew Marvell, Thomas Hardy and all the rest, telling myself that I didn't need any wretched, stupid coursework poets in order to know that I'd blown my chances with Nick.

I left for school at the same time as Kate but came back later, after Mum and Dad had gone to work, drew the curtains and spent the whole day watching DVDs. I knew I'd be in trouble for missing my test, but I didn't care. I watched everything I could lay my hands on – not just the good films but the ones I wouldn't normally bother with, like cowboy films, and Mum's Robert Redford films, and gory murders, and kooky situation comedies staring people like Meg Ryan.

To begin with they cheered me up. But, as the day progressed, their storylines began to grate, and so did all their pretty faces with their button noses, bright eyes and high, tight cheekbones. I saw them going through the motions with the smoothness of practitioners, yet nothing I watched that day had the taste and touch of real life. Nothing scraped the surface of the passion I'd seen in Finland when Rhys and Marika kissed, or the grief I'd seen at Lucy Chan's funeral. Why I was watching, I'd no idea.

In the end, I switched off the telly and went up the garden to sit in the log shelter and look out over the town. From there, you can usually see the rooftops of Newport all the way from the sea to the road bridge over the estuary. But it was raining that day, the clouds so low that it was hard to even see the end of Goat Street. I sat there smoking cigarettes and hoping they'd give me lung cancer and that would be the end of me.

Rain dropped onto me through the slats in the shelter roof, but I didn't move, and I was still there when Mum returned from work. She glanced up the garden from the kitchen window, and there I was, wet through, a stub of soggy cigarette hanging out of my mouth. I didn't even pretend I'd been in school. Mum frogmarched me indoors so that the neighbours wouldn't hear, then started laying into me. What was up with me? What could I be thinking of? Had I missed my English test? Had I been to school at all? *Did I have a brain inside my head?*

It wasn't just my day off school that got her going. Apparently, someone from her work had seen me mucking about with a boy in the cinema – which meant that my cover story last night about going for a long walk in the dark, 'in order to think', and getting lost, had been completely blown.

'*A boy!*' Mum said, as if the opposite sex were something that had landed from a distant planet bearing strange diseases. 'How's a night in the cinema with *a boy* going to get you through your tests? And is that why you took the day off school? Have you been with him? And why are you smoking? Don't tell me it's your first time, because I know you're lying. You do know, don't you, where it'll all end up? I've told you before – even a couple of puffs can be too much!'

I hoped it would. I really did. After that, my life wasn't worth living. Responding to this mere whisper of a boy in my life, Mum decided to mount guard on me. You'd have thought I was some rich financier's daughter in danger of a kidnap plot. She got Dad to drive me to school every day, 'just to make sure that she gets there', and rearranged her working hours so that she'd always be home by the time I returned.

'Who'd be a mother?' she kept on saying. But, in a funny sort of way, I reckoned she was enjoying herself.

Finally, she'd got me in her grip. She made up all sorts of rules about where I went, and how long for, and which of my friends were suitable and which were leading me astray. By the time that she had finished, hardly anyone was left.

'I'm going round to Rebecca's,' I'd say.

'You can't,' Mum would reply. 'She never does any work, and she's a bad influence.'

'I'm going round to Jody's.'

'Her parents won't be there. I don't trust you. You could get up to anything.'

'I'm going round to Jenna's.'

'Her parents give her too much freedom. You're staying put.'

As for Nick — I tried telling Mum I had no plans to see him ever again, but she wouldn't listen. I meant it, though. A week or so after our date, I saw Nick on the street and tried to smile, but he looked the other way.

After that, I hated him. Who did he think he was, Mr Takeaway himself, with his plans to make millions before the age of thirty? The more I thought about it, the more relieved I felt that I'd seen him in his true light before it was too late. In detention for my missed test — forced to write an English essay on the subject of 'My Favourite Sonnet' — I let rip.

'I hate poetry,' I wrote. 'Who do those wretched poets think they are, writing stupid sonnets that no one wants to read, and expecting people to study them hundreds of years later? Only a man would have the nerve to do a thing like that. It's typical, it is. Self-centred bastards – that's what my Aunt Jane calls them. She hates the lot of them, even Carl. And I hate them too. I used to hope for Mr Right, but now I know I'm better off without him. Life sucks. It really does. You start out with high hopes but end up eaten by worms. That's what Andrew Marvell says in his stupid sonnet to his mistress. I mean, what do you get out of it all? What do you get for all your efforts in life? Some bloody poem, if you're lucky!'

Usually you get good marks in our school for writing rude things about men, because they're seen as the enemy of women and their careers. But, for some reason, my essay seemed to really bother my English teacher. She got me after class, a couple of days later, and asked if anything – like Lucy Chan's death, for example – might be playing on my mind. She even went so far as to suggest I might be in need of grief counselling – an idea that I found ridiculous and turned down emphatically.

Mum was mad at me when she found out, because she said that something was obviously up with me and it might have 'helped'. But helped with *what*? Lucy had been Kate's friend, not mine, and nobody had offered *her* counselling – a fact that made her mad as well, when she found out.

'How dare they offer it to her, not me!' she said.

'And do you think you need it?' Mum said.

'No,' Kate said.

'Well then,' Mum said.

None of this improved the atmosphere at home, where a day off school had turned into the drama of the century. Nor did it improve the atmosphere at school, where my English teacher said that, if I wasn't grieving, I had no excuse for falling behind with my coursework. Targets were set for me to meet and checklists of objectives to be achieved. And my other teachers got in on the act as well. My homework diary had to be signed on a daily basis, and Mum was encouraged to stay in regular touch by phone.

Everybody was happier now, except for me. Mum loved phoning to keep tabs on me, and the teachers felt as if they were achieving something. If my headaches had started up again, then that was my problem, not theirs. By the time that everybody had finished with me, I was organized to within an inch of my life. But I knew I had nobody to blame but myself. If I'd only gone to school that fateful Thursday morning and sat my wretched test, I'd have saved myself a whole lot of trouble.

I accepted my fate with as good a grace as I could muster. I could have fought it, but there didn't seem much point. To Mum and school, it must have looked as if their hard line was paying off. But they couldn't see what was going on inside of me.

Since working on the Mrs Marridge Project, I swear this was the lowest point. Once I'd been inspired, but now those days were over. I'd been a dreamer, with the will to make things happen, but now I was just an ordinary schoolgirl who didn't have it in her to fight for what she wanted, simply doing what people told her.

My spirit had been broken, and it showed in everything I did. I knew what I was capable of when I wrote my boring essays and handed them in on time. But what was the point of doing anything else?

The strong-arm tactics were working, I suppose. They were turning me into the person everybody wanted me to be. Not that the rise in my grades meant anything to me personally. Home and school might be pleased with what I was achieving on their behalf, but I never felt as if I was achieving anything on *my* behalf. It was *their* education system, not mine. Their gain, my pain. Their glory. Their success.

Over the next couple of months, I inhabited a strange, dull limbo land where nothing seemed to touch me. Once I'd thought I had something to work towards, but now I knew how wrong I was. I'd been a fool for thinking somebody like me could ever fall in love and marry. What a joke! I mean, I couldn't even pull off a single date!

Mum and Dad might be relieved, but they didn't have a clue what was really going on. The only even remote pleasure I got any more came from surfing the net on Dad's computer, down in his office. Like a lonely wanderer on high seas, I'd go where the keyboard led me, tapping in random words and phrases and seeing where I ended up.

It was the only bit of freedom that I had. Maybe I wasn't interested in the banana trade, or conjuring, or how to make a bomb, but at least the choices were my own. Under the pretext of doing research for school, I wrote lonely letters to strangers in high places – the US president, Bob Geldof, the Archbishop of Canterbury – and read book reviews, lonely heart ads, Greenpeace fact sheets about rainforests and wacky information about UFOs. At a click, it was all there and, at a click, it was gone.

At one point, I even had a go at registering with a teenage dating line – not because I wanted a boyfriend, I hasten to add, but simply because I was curious. I gave my online name as SadLady, but that was taken, so I thought again and came up with LadyNile, which was Elin spelt backwards. I said that I was eighteen, dressed out of Top Shop, loved Justin Timberlake and hated Burberry. None of this was particularly true, but then neither were the replies I got, giving the impression that every boy online was six foot tall, blond-haired, hazel-eyed, had a terrific body and a wall full of snowboarding awards.

In the meantime, the spring term came and went. Kate and I still weren't exactly friends, but at least things were easier between us now that her mocks were over and a crop of good results had cheered her up. Everybody, it seemed, was in a better mood these days. Mum and Dad because they'd got tabs on me; Grandad because, having got no further with Mrs Morris, he'd joined some luncheon club where you could meet old ladies; Jane because Imogen's first teeth were through and she wasn't crying so much at night; and even Carl, who had somehow managed to wheedle his way back into favour.

Only I found it hard to cheer up. Spring heralded its arrival with a garden full of daffodils, but it made no difference. One weekend, I caught a glimpse of Rhys and Marika driving past in the family pickup truck. It was the first time I'd seen them since the wedding and they didn't look like royalty any more. They looked like students home for the holidays and, although I know this is ridiculous, I found it amazingly depressing.

The magic of the wedding had gone, replaced by ordinary life. And that was fine for them, I reckoned, because they probably didn't want to live out their years on some mountaintop, breathing rarefied thin air. But it wasn't fine for me, because I wanted something to believe in that was dizzying and wonderful. Wanted something to hope for that rose above the ordinary. Wanted my inspiration back, and everything that came with it.

I turned to the Internet, feeling sorry for myself and beaming lonely messages to anyone out there who might be bothered to answer, asking things like, 'Is it normal to be afraid of sex?', 'What is love?', 'Are all men jerks?' and 'Is the Age of Romance dead?'

I got all sorts of weird and wacky replies, wished I hadn't asked, and even considered changing my email address. Before I took that drastic step, however, I got an email from Melvin. I thought of binning it without reading it, but at least it didn't come attached to some stupid poser's name that couldn't possibly be true. You had to be a pretty regular sort of guy, I reckoned, to own up to 'Melvin'.

The message, when I opened it, was short and to the point. It was headed SWANS. 'In answer to your question,' it said, 'romance isn't dead. Wild swans mate for life – if you want to know what love is, you should look at them.'

MELVIN
MELVIN
MELVIN
MELVIN
MELVIN
MELVIN

* *
* Part VI *
* The Real Thing *
* *
* *
*

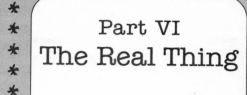

MELVIN MELVIN MELV MELVIN
MELVIN
MELVIN

Melvin

MEL
MELV
IN
MELVIN
MELVIN
MELVIN

MELVIN

MELVIN

16

Melvin

I emailed back and Melvin and I developed a friendship that brought the daffodils out in my life, if you
know what I mean. I started cautiously because I didn't
know if I could ever trust another boy – and, besides,
everybody knows that you have to be careful who you
pick up on the Internet.

But over time I started trusting Melvin, and he started
trusting me. Despite the computer screen between us,
we found ourselves going heart to heart and mind to
mind, nothing getting in the way.

In no time at all, I felt as if Melvin knew me better
than anybody else. Give or take a few minor details –
like my marriage project, for example, and the fact
that, unlike Melvin, I wasn't eighteen – he knew
everything about me; what I liked and what I didn't –
the whole truth, because what did I have to lose?

I knew the whole truth about him too – everything
you could ever want to know, right down to the
obscure TV programmes that he watched late into the

night, and his favourites bands, and things like that. In the end, we even had our 'own' band, the Seven Inches, whom I'd thought nobody had ever heard of until Melvin came along, insisting that their songs were modern classics.

He was like that, Melvin. His taste was immaculate. Yet for all the stuff he knew, he hated the education system, which – he said – had nothing to do with real life. The way he put it, we might just as well chuck all schooling and go on the Internet, where we'd learn twice as much. Either that, or go off travelling and discover things for ourselves.

That sounded great to me, and we started fantasizing about where we'd like to go together. I wasn't sure about Thailand after the tsunami, but Melvin reckoned it would be fine. He talked about the Aegean Sea, making it sound amazing, and said he wanted to take me to the Caribbean because he'd spent part of his childhood there.

For my part, I didn't care. Given the opportunity, I would have gone anywhere as long as Melvin went as well. He might still be in school, but already he'd done so much with his life. His family wasn't like mine, who either Euro-camped in France, travelling cheaply there and back by ferry, or spent their summer holidays at home and saved the money for their daughters' educations. Melvin's parents hacked through rainforests, climbed mountains, lived in jungle camps and ate armadillos. And I knew he wasn't making it up, because he sent me photographs of all the places that they'd been.

He knew so much as well – the mating habits of wild swans were only the start of it. 'I can't believe that you want to be my friend,' I wrote. 'I must seem so incredibly boring. All I've ever done in life is sit around worrying about brain tumours and dying.'

Melvin wrote back asking what I meant, and I explained about the asterisks in my diary. There'd been loads of them recently. Most had been to do with headaches, but only the other night I'd experienced a pain down my arm that could have been writer's cramp, given the amount of school work I was doing, but could equally have been the onset of a heart attack.

When I explained this to Melvin, I thought he would make fun of me. But he couldn't have been sweeter, emailing back to say he used to be like that himself, but then one day he'd realized that the only thing wrong with him was *worrying* about things being wrong with him!

'After that,' he wrote, 'I swear I never had another pain.'

That rang a bell. I threw away my diary and felt better for it immediately. Melvin emailed me a big 'Well done', saying that I wasn't just a mindless victim of fate but a strong, intelligent individual who had taken the first, all-important step to shaping her own destiny. I loved it when he wrote like that. Life suddenly felt on the up. Not all men, it seemed, were self-centred bastards. Thanks to Melvin, I had something to look forward to apart from school and death.

And so things might have remained – if Mum and I hadn't got into a major row. It was her fault, not mine. You'd have thought she had nothing to grumble about, given all the school work I was doing. But Mum without grumbles is like fish without chips, and when she found some undelivered letters in the bottom of my school bag, she went ballistic.

I'd forgotten that they were there, and hadn't thought they were important anyway – just stuff about summer fêtes and nominations for the PTA. But Mum saw them differently. She marched into my room and thrust them at me.

'What are *these*?' she said.

'They look like letters,' I replied.

'Don't you get funny with me!' Mum said. 'There are *ten* letters here, all addressed to *me* and *none* of them has ever been delivered. If I've told you once I've told you a hundred times – hanging on to letters with my name on them amounts to *theft*. Do you understand what I'm saying? *Are you listening?*'

Of course I was listening – Mum was yelling so

loudly that I couldn't possibly do anything else! I said that I was sorry, but it didn't work. What really got Mum going was the fact that the letters included an invitation to a careers convention in school — *last week*. In other words, we had missed it. I tried to smooth things over by saying it didn't matter, but that only made things worse.

'You stupid, stupid, *stupid girl*!' Mum yelled. 'If finding the right career doesn't matter, I don't know what does. What's happened to your ambition? You used to want to be an astronaut. You used to want to be a doctor. You used to want to make something of yourself! *What's come over you?*'

How was I to answer that? I flushed and muttered something about, 'That was then — now I've got better things to do.'

'Oh yes?' Mum said. 'Like what?'

'*Like getting married,*' I replied.

The words came as a shock — to me as much as to Mum. I didn't mean to say them. What I meant to say was 'like travelling', but they just came bursting out. Mum reeled back in a state of shock. So did I. We stared at each other and, for a moment, you could have heard a pin drop. Then Mum asked, in a small, shocked voice, '*What did you just say?*'

There was no way I could turn back the clock. Besides, I *did* want to get married. It hadn't been a slip of the tongue. I'd said it because I meant it. All this time I'd thought that I was finished with the Mrs Marridge Project. But it hadn't finished with me. *Far from it.*

'What's wrong with marriage?' I heard myself saying, as if this was something that Mum and I had to have out sometime and we might as well do it now. 'It must have something going for it, otherwise people wouldn't do it. Even divorced people go out and get married again. Even rich people, who have to go to all the trouble of drawing up pre-nuptial agreements. I mean, gay people want to get married, and film stars who are so beautiful that they could have anyone. And the papers are always going on about Prince Charles marrying Camilla Parker Bowles. So why shouldn't I get married too?'

Mum stared at me helplessly. 'Because you're *young*,' she said, as if pointing out the obvious. 'Because you're smart and bright, and you've got your whole life ahead of you. Because this is *your time*, and you should be enjoying it. Because you'll never be so *free* again, or have so many *choices*.'

That was rich, coming from a mother whose idea of freedom was sitting GCSEs! I burst out laughing. I simply couldn't help myself. Mum didn't get it, did she?

'Once upon a time,' I said, 'girls my age were married already and had families. You should read your history books. Once there were no teenagers, only women. And I'm a woman, Mum. You still think I'm a child. You think I'm the little girl with white cuffs in the family photo on the wall. But I'm old enough to have babies and you don't seem to realize it.'

Mum blanched. 'Are you telling me you're *pregnant*?' she said.

I wished I was, just to shock her, but I shook my head. Her relief was visible – but it didn't stop her laying in to me.

'*Once upon a time*,' she said furiously, 'the women who didn't die young in childbirth had so many babies that they ended up dead anyway, long before their time. Their lives were unspeakably hard. They had no rights. Their husbands owned them, body and soul. They couldn't say they'd had enough and just walk out. They couldn't vote. Didn't have an education. Didn't have the chances you have to make something of yourself – *and are you telling me that's what you want?*'

It was such a ridiculous question that I refused to reply. Not that I had much chance, because Mum started on about the battles women had fought to give girls like me freedom of choice.

'I'm only trying to exercise my freedom of choice,' I said, when I finally got a word in edgeways.

'Don't be a smart aleck!' Mum replied.

'Better than being a control freak,' I said.

'You're an insult to your sex,' she replied.

'At least I don't kid myself,' I said. 'At least there's no pretence. I'm not living a pseudo-married life, pretending to be an independent woman when I'm really *just like all the other wives!*'

That put the lid on it. Mum stormed out of the room, taking all ten precious letters with her, and the row was over. I had had the last word, but it brought no satisfaction. How was I ever going to face her again – or Dad either, for that matter – having poured scorn on the way they chose to live their lives?

That night, after everyone had gone to bed, I crept down to Dad's office and emailed Melvin. I was desperate to get his opinion. 'I'm telling you this,' I wrote, 'because everybody will find out soon enough, and I want you to know first. I mean, Mum's bound to tell Dad, and then Kate'll hear – if she hasn't heard already – and tell all her friends. And Jane'll hear, and have a good old laugh with Carl, and Grandad will find out, and probably Jenna, Jody and Rebecca. The whole town will find out, and I'll be a laughing stock because I haven't even got a boyfriend, and I'm useless with the opposite sex anyway.

'The thing is, I want to get married. It's something I've wanted ever since I was little, but I've only realized it recently. I want it more than anything, even travelling to the Caribbean, and a million times more than some stupid job, pulling teeth like Jenna's mum, or working so hard, like her dad, that I end up having a heart attack. It's hard to explain, but I think it's all to do with feeling safe inside. With knowing that I'm loved, no matter what I say or do. I want someone who won't nag me, and will always stand by me – not because I'm good enough, or clever enough, but because I'm *me*.

'So what do you think?' I finished off. 'Am I stupid, like Mum says? I really need to know, so please write back. I mean, I could be crazy for all I know. So give it to me straight. Don't be afraid. I want the truth.'

That email was the closest I'd ever come to opening up to anyone. When I'd finished, I sat in front of the screen for ages before I dared send it off. Then I sat for ages afterwards, wondering what I'd done and waiting for a reply.

I didn't get one – at least, not then – and eventually went up to bed, worried that I never would. But next morning, in the computer room at school, I found a message in my inbox. I double-clicked it open. My heart was thudding and I felt sick. What I dreaded more than anything was Melvin being polite, just for the sake of not hurting my feelings. But I obviously didn't know him very well. He couldn't have been more direct and to the point.

'You're NOT crazy,' he wrote. 'You're NOT stupid. There's NOTHING wrong with you. You ask me to give it to you straight, Elin, so here goes. You're a VERY SPECIAL person and I'm mad about you. We're made for each other. I hope that you can see it. I'm glad you want to marry, because I do too. I want to marry you. WILL YOU MARRY ME? I await your reply.'

17

Engaged!

You wouldn't believe how long it took to come up with a simple answer to a simple question that only required a 'yes'. I'd been waiting for months now for something like this. It had been my dream. Everything I'd done had been in preparation for it. But now I couldn't have found myself frozen into a greater state of immobility if I'd been some sheep petrified by a dog.

Melvin emailed again. Several times. To begin with, he didn't mention his proposal but kept things light and chatty. But when I still didn't reply, he started pressing me.

'We're meant for each other,' he wrote. 'Loners both of us. You know I'm right.'

Perhaps I did. I'd never actually thought of myself as a loner before, but perhaps life had turned me into one. After all, I hardly ever saw my friends outside of school any more. And, when I did, I couldn't think of anything to say to them. I mean, what was there to talk about except for work?

The Real Thing

I hardly spoke to anyone at home either. Since our row, Mum and I had scarcely said a word to each other. If I wanted to eat, she cooked for me. If my clothes needing washing, she'd load them into the machine with everybody else's. If I needed toothpaste or shampoo, she put it on the shopping list. But if I wanted to ignore her, then that was fine by her too.

Things weren't much better between Dad and me. A few days after my big row with Mum, I discovered he'd phoned school about my seeing that counsellor. I was furious, and we had a major row that ended up with my not speaking to him either.

This left only Kate. I longed for us to be friends again, but her A levels were almost upon her, which meant that she was home on study leave, shut in her bedroom not speaking to a soul. Poor old Kate. If I'd been on study leave, I'd be sunbathing in the garden or on the beach, making the most of my little bit of freedom. And so would she, once upon a time. But she had changed and if it hadn't been for Melvin, out there on the World Wide Web, I wouldn't have had a single friend in the family.

Even so, I didn't reply. I was terrified of discovering that I'd misread the intention of his emails and he hadn't actually meant to propose to me. In other words, that he'd only done it because he felt sorry for me.

So I went to school and came home again, did a bit

of homework, watched a bit of telly and spent the remaining hours in my bedroom, mostly staring into space. Melvin emailed again, saying I was the only one who understood him and could I please email back to let him know that I was all right. He was obviously worried, but the more emails I received, and the more I wanted to reply, the less able I found myself to do so.

Even when Melvin sent those photographs of himself and his family on holiday, I didn't reply. His tanned, friendly face came as a surprise. I hadn't expected him to be good-looking as well as kind, understanding and in love with me. That had been too much to hope for. And yet he was.

But *still* I didn't reply.

'At least let me know you're alive,' he wrote. 'Even if you don't want to email any more. Even if my proposal has freaked you out. Or if your parents disapprove. At least let me know – at least do that.'

After that, I received a whole string of email cards with red roses on them, each one coming with the message 'I'm crazy about you' and a little tune. I deleted them all and wept over each one.

Summer had arrived outside my window, but it was incapable of raising my spirits. The end of May had always been my favourite time of year, the trees newly green and studded with white flowers like bridal bouquets. But this year was different. My whole life felt like a GCSE exam that was about to go wrong and there was nothing I could do to stop it. I told myself that everything would work out if I only pulled myself together, but I knew it wasn't true.

One lunchtime at school, I found a final email waiting in my inbox. 'If I don't get a reply, then you'll never hear from me again,' Melvin wrote. 'I'll give you three days, then I'll delete your email address and never bother you again.'

Still I didn't reply! I wanted to, believe me. I'd worked out by now that Melvin really did love me and wasn't acting out of pity. And I loved him too. I was sure of that. But I still held back. For the awful truth was that I wasn't old enough to marry. No way near it. *And Melvin didn't know that yet!*

'If he finds out I'm not eighteen, he'll dump me,' I thought. 'I can't tell him I lied. Can't tell him I'm only fourteen. I mean, how can I own up to a thing like that?'

One day went by, then two days, then a whole string more. I was done for and I knew it. It was the worst week of my life. To make matters worse, Jenna, Jody and Rebecca decided to gang up on me about my odd behaviour.

'We're worried about you,' they said. 'You've gone so quiet and look so miserable. Something's wrong. Why won't you talk?'

I wished I could – but the only person I could really talk to had just deleted my address from his inbox! Not that I could explain that to my girlfriends. With irritating persistence, they refused to give up on me. Every break they were determinedly 'there for me', and every lunchtime they took me off to town, trying to lure me back to life with treats and outings. I wished that I had study leave like Kate and could get away from them. My only hope of happiness, I knew, was an email from Melvin, but that wasn't going to happen.

I checked my inbox daily, though, hoping he'd have changed his mind. But my only emails came from Jenna, Jody and Rebecca, saying things like 'Hi – how's it going?', 'Life is meant for more than work' and 'Do you want to go shopping on Saturday?' There was never anything from Melvin.

At the end of a week, I decided to stop looking. But a couple of days later I thought I'd go online one final time, then if there was nothing I'd know that was that. I waited until the house was quiet and everyone had gone to bed, then I crept down to Dad's office and switched on the computer.

Once its familiar hum had seemed full of promise and excitement, but now it sounded mechanical and dead. I sat before the screen feeling bleak and lonely, knowing, before I even looked, that my inbox would be empty. But I was wrong. One single email was waiting for me.

From Melvin.

'It's no good,' he wrote. 'I can't do this. I really miss you, Elin. I can't live my life without you. Even if you don't want to marry me, can't we still be friends?'

I answered on the spot. No holding back this time. No mindless dithering. I knew a chance like this would never come along again.

'ireallymissyoutoo,' I typed back on fingers that could scarcely get the words down fast enough. 'icantlivewithoutyoueither. howcouldieverpossibly? ofcourseiwill. illmarryyou.'

soon . . .
even sooner

9.30 9.30 9.30 9.30

Part VII
Study Leave

nine – thirty
Fishguard
ferry terminal

where the hell have u been??

18
Caught out

From that moment onwards, I was engaged. What I felt for Melvin was almost a religious thing. I would have done anything for him. Would have followed him to the ends of the earth. Now that I'd answered 'yes', my life felt complete. I loved Melvin 'to the depth and breadth and height my soul can reach', to quote another of my English coursework poets – not a wretched man this time, but Elizabeth Barrett Browning.

At long last, my Mrs Marridge Project made sense. It had a purpose – and that purpose was Melvin. He was what I'd worked for, writing in secret in my room, cutting articles out of newspapers, making lists and charts and storing essays in my secret marriage course-work folder down at the house on the estuary. Every-thing I'd done, from checking house prices to trying my hand at cooking and practising my DIY skills, had been for him.

Now all we had to do was *meet*! A flurry of emails back and forth that night simply wasn't enough. We couldn't wait to set eyes on each other. Nothing must be allowed to get in our way. Not school, or exams, or our parents, or what our friends had to say. Not all the miles between London, where he lived down at the end of the Northern Line in Morden, and me in Wales.

'*Soon*,' I wrote to Melvin.

'*Even sooner*,' he wrote back.

Coming down for breakfast the following morning, I felt transformed. I was a Woman of Maturity at last and expected everybody to notice the change. But no one noticed anything, too busy talking about boring things like what time Dad would be in tonight, and who would do the shopping, and who would cook.

'That's families for you,' I wrote to Melvin during break at school. 'Breakfast was my engagement party and no one knew it except me. And, do you know what – I *loved* the secrecy! It made me feel so powerful. It made me feel in charge, even if nobody knew it.'

Melvin emailed that he knew just what I meant. There was something about a secret, he wrote, especially one shared. We planned to meet, but didn't tell a soul. *Soon* was our catchword, but it couldn't be soon enough. Melvin was all for jumping on the next train, and wanted me to do the same, meeting halfway between London and west Wales. But I knew I'd never get away with it, not this weekend, which was going to be a big one on the revision front, what with Kate's first A level on Monday morning and my first end-of-year exam. Mum would be on my case, which meant that my first real opportunity to do what I wanted would be Monday morning after leaving the house for school.

In the end I arranged to meet Melvin at nine-thirty, down at Fishguard ferry terminal, where we'd take a Sea Cat day trip to Ireland and damn the stupid end-of-year exams. The trip was my idea. I thought the Sea Cat would be more romantic than trailing round somewhere like Bristol, looking at shops. Mum and Dad would think I was in school, and I'd be home again before they realized otherwise. The fact that there'd be questions asked about my absence from the French exam was something I'd worry about later.

How I got through that weekend, I've no idea. By Sunday night, I was in a total state. Nothing mattered in my life except for Monday morning and meeting Melvin. I decided to go to bed early in the hope of sleeping long and waking up fresh and beautiful.

But first I had to sort out my clothes.

This was no easy matter. A bride preparing for her wedding couldn't have worried more about what to wear. The simple truth was that I knew the books that Melvin read, his favourite music, his favourite TV programmes and his deepest hopes and aspirations. But I didn't know the first thing about his taste in clothes.

I emailed him about what to wear, but he said it really didn't matter. 'Surprise me,' he said – which sent me into a spin because I couldn't find what I'd done with that article 'DRESS TO IMPRESS ON YOUR FIRST DATE'.

Not that this was going to be an ordinary first date. Wearing high-heeled boots because they made me look sexier simply wasn't what it was about. I tried everything that night, hoping to achieve the desired effect of surprising Melvin while reflecting something of my true nature.

It was a difficult balancing act, to put it mildly. I worked my way from jeans to skirts, dresses to smart jackets, sloppy sweaters to my red velvet dress. But however many clothes I tried on, I knew that the real surprise of the day was going to be my age.

It was enough to make anybody panic. I stood in front of the mirror, staring at my stick-thin body, knowing that Melvin would realize straight away that I was only fourteen. Inside I might be a Woman of Maturity but outside – where it showed – I was just some little girl who'd strung him along.

'I'm going to have to come clean,' I thought. 'I'm going to have to tell him I'm not old enough to marry, before he finds out for himself!'

This was all very well. But how do you tell a boy – especially one who's engaged to you – that you're too young to marry him with or without parental consent; to buy him a drink; vote; drive a car; apply for a passport or credit card without your parents' permission; and have sex with him without putting him in danger of prison?

That night, I lay awake trying to compose a '*Dear Melvin, I'm so sorry . . .*' letter that I could email off to him before he embarked on a long and fruitless journey. I tried countless different ways of explaining myself, but none of them sounded right and I didn't send them. It would be nice to say that honesty got the better of me, but at two-thirty in the morning my mobile rang.

'Hi, Elin, is that you?' a voice said, exploding into my life and giving me such a shock that at first I couldn't answer.

It was Melvin. A living, breathing real Melvin too – not some emailed photograph or a string of words on a screen. A Melvin with a voice – and I only had to hear that voice to know that there was *no way* I could ever admit to lying to him!

'Hi,' I answered shakily.

'Hi,' he said again. 'Elin, that *is* you?'

'Melvin?' I said.

'You're real!' he said.

'So are you!' I said.

'I love you,' he said.

'I love you too,' I said.

'I can't wait to see you.'

'I can't wait to see *you*.'

'At the ferry terminal . . .'

'On the platform where the London train comes in . . .'

'I can't wait . . .'

'I'll be there waiting . . .'

'I love you.'

'I love you too.'

'Goodbye. See you tomorrow.'

'See you tomorrow. Goodbye.'

That was it – our first real conversation. I cradled the phone long after Melvin had gone, nursing the embers of his presence and thinking of the millions of fascinating things I could have said but hadn't.

'When we're old,' I thought, 'we'll remember that conversation and laugh about it, and think how young and silly we were. But we'll know that, from this moment onwards, for richer, for poorer, in sickness and in health, we always had each other and we always had our love.'

After that, there were no worries about clothes, or even about lying. Before I fell asleep, I texted Melvin, saying, 'I'll see you in the morning.' He texted back, saying, 'I'm on my way already. On the night bus to the station, to catch the first train out of London – see you at nine-thirty,' to which I texted back, swearing on poor old innocent, unsuspecting Mum's life that I'd be on that platform waiting when his train came in.

Then I closed my eyes and slept like a baby. You'd have thought I'd toss and turn, but I couldn't have slept better if tomorrow was the first day of study leave and I didn't have another lesson for the rest of term.

Next morning, Kate was up before me, looking nervous about her German oral exam. Mum cooked a special breakfast, which neither of us could eat, then Dad drove us both to school and dropped us off at the gate, never knowing that my bursting school bag wasn't full of books but of clothes and make-up.

Kate and I walked up the drive together, friends for once. When we parted at the sixth-form block, she wished me well for my exam, and I wished her well for hers. 'You'll do fine,' I said, a big lump in my throat. You'd have thought I was never going to see my sister again.

'So will you,' she said – and I hoped that she was right!

Once Kate had gone, I turned my back on school and darted back down the drive from tree to tree, hoping nobody would notice my strange behaviour. My plan was to change my clothes in the town loo, then hotfoot down to the ferry terminal. But the toilets were locked, so I had to go straight to the ferry terminal, hoping to change there instead.

It was a long walk downhill, all the way along a busy main road, and I felt painfully conspicuous in my school uniform. I hoped that nobody I knew would see me and guess that I was bunking. I also hoped that I would be on time. In the distance, I could see the Sea Cat coming in from Ireland, moving at an amazing speed. One minute it was just a dot on the horizon and the next it was the biggest thing in view – a great white slice of triple-tiered wedding cake served on a sea-blue plate.

Before I'd even reached the terminal it had berthed, and people and cars were pouring off. I ran along the seafront in a panic. A train was in as well, and I guessed that it was the London train and I was late. Probably Melvin was waiting on the platform, wondering where I was.

I reached the terminal and headed straight for the London platform. But the place was full of backpackers off the Sea Cat, families with little kids and luggage, and gangs of lads back from a beery weekend in Ireland. I could scarcely move, let alone see Melvin anywhere.

I stood against a wall, waiting for the crowd to subside, hoping that our eyes would meet across the throng, like Romeo and Juliet. But the only eyes I met belonged to a loser in an ill-fitting suit, whose pained expression suggested toothache, and an old man in a mac, who smelt like a drain.

They looked me up and down, and I looked away quickly, knowing you can't be too careful these days because there are some funny people out there in the world. The loser wandered off, but the mac-man remained. I could see him out of the corner of my eye – and he was still looking my way.

Where was Melvin? I started down the London platform, but it seemed to me that the mac-man was following. I glanced back a couple of times and managed not to catch his eye, but he was always somewhere behind me. In a growing state of anxiety, I pulled out my mobile. Perhaps I'd got it wrong about the London train. Perhaps the train in front of me had come from somewhere else and Melvin hadn't arrived yet. Certainly I couldn't see him anywhere.

I checked for messages, in case there'd been a hold-up and he'd texted me. But my inbox was empty. Then I dialled Melvin's number and his phone rang and rang. Why wasn't he answering? What had happened to him? And why was that old man still following me?

In the end, Melvin answered. 'Where are you?' he said.

'What d'you mean, *where am I*?' I cried down the phone. 'I'm on the platform, where I said I'd be.'

'So am I, but I don't see you. Are you sure you're on the London platform?' Melvin said.

'Of course I am,' I said.

'Tell me where you're standing,' Melvin said.

'Under the Departures screen,' I said.

'I still don't see you,' Melvin said. 'What are you wearing?'

What *was* I wearing? *Oh, my God!* I felt the dead weight on my shoulder of a school bag full of clothes. *How could I possibly have forgotten to put them on?* Or to do my hair or make-up? And how was I going to explain to Melvin that the blushing little schoolgirl with the scrubbed face and scraggy hair, standing under the Departures screen, was the wife-to-be he'd come all this way to find?

I turned away, hoping he hadn't realized yet that I was me. No longer was I waiting for that moment when our eyes met. I looked in the opposite direction and met the mac-man's eyes instead. He came heading straight towards me. What did he want? I didn't like him. I tried to walk away, but he followed me, bringing his smell with him.

'Melvin . . .' I called down the phone. But the line was dead. Melvin couldn't help me. I was alone. The mac-man came and stood in front of me, blocking my path and fixing me with a determined gaze. He smiled as if he actually knew me personally – and suddenly a truly awful thought occurred to me.

He couldn't be . . .

It wasn't possible . . .

The man in front of me – he couldn't by some weird, freaky, cruel twist of fate be . . .

'*Melvin?*' I said.

A voice behind me answered, 'Yes.' I turned around, only to find the loser in the suit standing there clutching a bunch of daffodils. 'These are for you,' he said, thrusting them at me, big beads of sweat standing out on his forehead.

The world was going mad! I backed away from him – away from both of them. I'd had enough. I really had. 'If you don't leave me alone, I'll call the police!' I said.

'But they're your favourite flowers,' the loser said.

How he knew that, I didn't know. 'I don't want your stupid daffodils!' I shouted, in a state of total panic. 'I'm waiting for a friend! *Go away, and leave me alone!*'

The loser flushed. 'I *am* that friend,' he said.

'Don't be so stupid,' I said.

'You *are* Elin?' he said.

'What if I am?' I said.

'*I'm Melvin,*' he said.

You could have knocked me dead. Dimly I was aware of the mac-man rattling his tin at me, demanding loose change, then, when he had no luck, moving on down the platform. But already he was yesterday's news. I was too busy staring at the loser with his pained expression, beads of sweat and terrible suit, taking in the fact that it was actually physically possible that he *could* be Melvin. He was the right sort of age, give or take a year or so, and he knew my name and liking for daffodils.

But, even so, I refused to believe it. 'I'm sorry, I misheard you,' I said.

The loser flushed. 'I'm Melvin,' he said again.

How I kept from bursting into tears, I just don't know. The nervous young man in front of me was nothing like the carefree boy in the photograph. He was a different shape altogether. Different hair, different everything. That boy had been tanned, but this one's face was pasty. He had a crop of small pink spots around his mouth, whereas the other Melvin, the real Melvin as I thought of him – *my Melvin* – was smooth-skinned and unblemished. He was sleek, but the loser in front of me was stocky, to put it mildly. Instead of having a shock of golden hair, his mousy-coloured offering was cut so short that I could see through to his scalp.

I had been duped. There were funny people out there in the world and you couldn't be too careful these days. That's what I'd already told myself, and now my words came back to haunt me. What a fool I'd been! What a naïve little idiot! All this time I'd been worrying my head off about my one little lie, but Melvin had told a pack of them.

Suddenly I could see the whole thing. The whole

deception from beginning to end. This pathetic boy in front of me had never hacked through rainforests or grown up in the Caribbean. He'd never holidayed in jungle huts and eaten armadillo. He wasn't the Melvin he'd pretended to be, and I didn't know who I despised more – him for deceiving me or me for falling for it.

'*Liar!* You're a liar and I hate you!' I cried, and turn-ed and ran away from him.

Melvin ran after me, still clutching his stupid daffodils, pleading with me to come back. People stopped and stared at us. We tore outside, leaving the ferry terminal behind. Melvin caught up with me and tried to grab my arm, but I cried 'Don't touch me!' with such venom that he flushed, offended, and said I needn't worry, he wasn't the sort of boy who'd force himself on girls – especially *little schoolkids* like me!

'I'm not the only one who's lied,' he said. 'I might have made a few things up, but when it comes to lying about age, you win the prize!'

In the end we both calmed down. We sat on the sea wall, not knowing what to do next. Melvin said that the whole thing could have been worse, and I agreed.

'You could have been that smelly tramp,' I said.

'And you could have been *anybody*,' he said, 'given that I picked you up on the Internet. I mean, the Internet!'

We both agreed it had been a stupid thing to do.

Melvin added that it had been pretty stupid to agree to meet as well. I tried to make light of the whole thing by saying that his biggest mistake had been to turn up in that suit.

'I wanted to look smart for you,' he said.

'You don't look smart. You look a prat,' I said.

'I know,' Melvin said, and managed a smile, as if the worst was over and he'd survived. He didn't look so bad when he wasn't frowning. Out in the sun, his face didn't look so pasty either, and his spots didn't bother me quite so much.

Not that anything changed the way I felt. He was still the wrong Melvin, as far as I was concerned, and I was still mad at him. I stared out to sea, thinking of what might have been. Why I didn't walk away, I just don't know. I thought about my French exam, which would be happening right now. What Melvin was thinking about, I'd no idea. He peeled out of his suit jacket and sat on the sea wall, seeming to draw comfort from the bright sun. Neither of us said a word to each other until one Sea Cat had gone and another was on its way in.

Then Melvin spoke at last. 'Look, what I think is this,' he said, getting to his feet and picking up his jacket. 'You've lied to me and I've lied to you, but it doesn't have to spoil the day. We could call it quits and do the sea trip anyway. Maybe neither of us is what the other expected, but we could still have a good time. We don't have to talk to each other, if we don't want. But we've both lost a day, and we might as well get something out of it. What do you think? We could do the round trip, see a bit of Ireland and still be back by the end of the afternoon. *What harm would it do?'*

19

In Good Hands

It was a seriously stupid idea. Absolutely crazy. Not for a split second did I think it made any remote kind of sense – so why I went along with it, I've no idea. The words came out of me as if they had a life of their own – 'Oh, why not?' and 'What the hell!' – as if they were nothing to do with me and someone else had spoken them.

Melvin looked surprised, as if he hadn't expected me to agree so readily. But he wasn't half as surprised as me! Maybe my disappointment had got the better of me, or maybe something reckless in my nature was struggling to get out. 'When I was young, I ran off with a man,' I'd always be able to say, dining out on the story into my old age. I wouldn't say, of course, that it had been the wrong man, with the wrong face, and a suit that didn't fit and spots around his mouth.

Even after we'd bought our tickets at the ferry terminal, and I'd found a loo at last and changed my clothes, I was still in a state of shock. We boarded the

Sea Cat, and I didn't know what had come over me. Nothing felt real any more, not until the moment when the Sea Cat edged out of the dock, and there, in the entrance to the harbour, it suddenly came to me that I had made the right decision. Beyond the wall, I could see blue water all the way to the horizon – a massive, inky sea with a turquoise sky above it and white gulls on the wing. I felt my spirits rise. Only a coward would turn their back on an adventure like this!

All the way to Ireland, that's what I told myself, sitting before a huge glazed window while the ocean rushed beneath me in a swell of white, churning water. I'd never been to Ireland before. Beyond the Sea Cat's destination, Rosslare, I didn't know the first thing about the landmass on the other side of the water, and I couldn't wait to take a look at it.

Melvin bought me food and drink, but apart from saying 'Thank you' I didn't take much notice of him. He tried to talk to me, but his real life didn't interest me. I didn't care that he had a cat, and lived at home, and had passed his driving test. Nor did I care that his ancestors had been Irish on one side and Vikings on the other, if you went back far enough – or that he'd never been as far as France, let alone the Caribbean.

Only when he lapsed into silence did I take any proper notice. He looked so sad and lonely, sitting there in his stupid suit, that I started to feel guilty for not bothering to listen. It wouldn't have taken much to show a bit of interest. For the first time, I thought about the real Melvin and *his* hopes and aspirations, which had all been dashed because I hadn't been the girl I'd said I was. I wished I could turn back the clock and that we could do the whole thing over again, only both of us telling the truth this time so that there'd be no cruel surprises.

Melvin caught me staring and said, 'What?'

'Was anything you told me true?' I said. 'I'm not trying to be funny. I just want to know.'

Melvin thought about it for a minute. 'I was always true about my feelings,' he said. 'I might have made some things up, but everything I said I felt was real. And the things that I believe, as well. Like education being stupid. I didn't make *that* up.'

Suddenly he sounded like the old Melvin again. I smiled ruefully, realizing for the first time that there was probably a bit of my real Melvin mixed up with the lies.

'Perhaps his deception wasn't so terrible, after all,' I thought. 'And mine wasn't either. Perhaps the strangers who met on the London platform weren't totally removed from our real selves.'

It was a startling idea and one that hadn't occurred to me until now.

'What are you thinking?' Melvin said.

'Nothing,' I said. 'Absolutely nothing.' But something in my attitude towards him had changed, and I realized it the moment the coast of Ireland appeared in the distance, and he pointed it out, his hand upon my shoulder – and I allowed it to linger before I shook it off. I felt its warmth and didn't mind.

I should have known then that I was sailing into trouble, but I didn't see it. I should have stayed on that Sea Cat when it docked and come straight back. But there was more to Ireland than the harbour at Rosslare, and more to Melvin than spotty skin and shaved hair – and suddenly it seemed worth exploring.

So when Melvin said, 'Look, I've got my driving licence on me – we could hire a car for a couple of hours,' I said it sounded like a brilliant idea.

Everything went well at first. Melvin said he wanted to show me the village where his ancestors came from, and I said that, as long as we didn't miss the Sea Cat home, that was fine by me. It *was* fine too. For a while, driving down the highway, I felt as if everything in my life had come together in a single thread – all the good things and the bad, the sad things and the happy ones, like diamonds on a necklace, and that necklace was the road, leading me off on a grand adventure.

But when we lost our way, the adventure didn't feel so grand. Melvin blamed the Irish road signs, but I blamed him for not taking my advice and buying a map. Finding the right village was proving impossible, but Melvin refused to give up.

He refused for hours, and wouldn't listen when I warned him that we really needed to turn back. The afternoon wound down and the sun started lowering over the hills, but he still wouldn't give up. We had reached a loch by now, and Melvin reckoned that his ancestral village was on the other side. He hired a boat, and I never should have gone with him, but he talked me into it.

'You'll really regret it if you don't,' he said. 'I mean, look how beautiful it is. Out in the middle of the loch, we'll get a fantastic view.'

And he was right. We didn't go out very far, because I made such a fuss, but the view of soft grey mountains rising from dark waters was spectacular. Melvin said he wished we didn't ever have to go back, and I said I knew how he felt – but I didn't mean it as much as him. I kept on thinking about the ferry timetable, and glancing at my watch and knowing I should have been home hours ago.

In the end, I finally persuaded him to turn back. He still hadn't found his precious village, but I'd managed to get through to him how much trouble I was in. We were a long way from the Sea Cat and an even longer way from home. Even as things stood, we'd be lucky to get back to Rosslare before darkness fell. The sun was lowering over the hills and the light fading, making everything around the loch look different. Places and distances were deceptive, and Melvin ended up steering the boat into the wrong harbour on the wrong side of the loch.

By the time we got back to the hire car, it was pitch dark. Even if we drove to Rosslare at a hundred miles an hour, I knew we'd missed the last Sea Cat home. I burst into tears and demanded that Melvin take me back to Rosslare anyway. But it had been a long day since his start in Morden at four in the morning, and he said he was too exhausted to even get behind the wheel.

The whole thing was a shambles. Melvin suggested we spend the night in one of the holiday cottages on the edge of the loch. But no way was I breaking and entering on top of everything else, so we spent the night at the local pub.

I felt safer there. Reluctantly – and a bit late in the day, you might think – I'd come to the conclusion that Melvin wasn't to be trusted. It was thanks to him that we were stranded, and I somehow got the feeling that it was no accident. What sort of person would have gone looking for a village he'd never been to before without even taking a map? And what sort of person would have taken us back to the wrong side of the loch?

I decided I didn't want to be on my own with Melvin and insisted on us having two single rooms. He pointed out that one would be cheaper but I refused to listen. I couldn't wait to go to bed and shut the door on him, but first there was the little matter of Mum and Dad to be sorted out. I simply didn't dare phone home and it even took courage to try Jenna instead. I failed to get her on my mobile, which had no reception, but had more success with the payphone in the lobby. Melvin stood over me while I was talking, listening in on everything I said.

'Jenna, thank God,' I burst out, as soon as she answered my call. 'You know you're always saying that you're there for me – well, I need you now. I need your help.'

'Elin, where *are* you?' Jenna answered. 'Your parents are off their heads. They're phoning everyone, but no one knows a thing.'

'I'm in Ireland,' I said.

'You're *where*?' Jenna said.

'I'll tell you everything when I get back,' I said. 'But, please, oh *please*, will you tell Mum and Dad that I'm all right? Do this one thing for me and I'll be in your debt for ever. I mean it, I really do. Don't say where I am, because I don't want Mum and Dad to be madder at me than they are already. And I promise, on my life, that I'll be back tomorrow morning.'

Jenna wasn't happy about this, to put it mildly. At first she said no way, but then, when she couldn't persuade me to talk to them myself, she reluctantly agreed on the condition that I came clean when I got back and told her *everything*. I thanked her a million times over.

'You *will* come back, won't you?' Jenna said.

'Cross my heart and hope to die,' I said.

'Are you all right?' she said.

Tears pricked my eyes. Where they'd come from I'd no idea, but I found I couldn't answer and Melvin had to take the phone from me and put it back on the cradle.

'You're fine,' he said. 'Your parents have nothing to worry about because you're safe with me. I give you my word. You'll be back in the morning. And, in the meantime, *you're in good hands*.'

20

Lost Without a Map

Good hands or not, Melvin still tried to force his way into my bedroom when we went up to bed. I was feeling more relaxed, having sorted out Mum and Dad, but no sooner had I fished my room key out of my pocket than he had to go and spoil things by sticking his foot in the door.

I pushed him out of the way.

'Why are you acting as if you don't trust me?' he said. 'I've bought you food, hired a boat, hired a car, put petrol in it and given you a good time – and now you pay me back by going cold on me. What's up with you? I thought that we were friends.'

He tried again, but I was too quick for him and slammed the door in his face. Before it shut, I caught a glimpse of a sullen, stolid expression that I hadn't seen before. I didn't like it. There was something nasty about it. Something mean and small.

'You're supposed to be engaged to me,' he whined through the boards between us.

I locked the door as well. 'I'm not supposed to be anything of the sort,' I said. 'That was someone else. It wasn't me. It was the person I pretended to be.'

After that, Melvin tried wheedling, bribery and threats, but nothing he said made any difference. I even wedged a chair under the door handle, just to be on the safe side, and in the end he gave up and let himself into his room next door. Here he banged around for hours, and I guessed he must be drinking because, at one point, I heard him throwing up.

I tried my best to ignore him, and thought about my family instead — Mum and Dad and Kate — and how much I loved them, and Jane and Grandad as well, and even Carl and Imogen Louise. I also thought about the Mrs Marridge Project and where it had brought me.

'Whoever would have imagined,' I asked myself, 'that when I had my epiphany at Lucy Chan's funeral, it'd all end up in some hotel bedroom holding a drunken stranger at bay?'

I thought how much I'd changed since those early days. I'd come a million miles from the impatient girl who could never let things 'just happen' but always had to have a strategy — short-term objectives, and long-term ones, and plans and lists, and things like that. Application had been my key, but application wouldn't help me now. It was just a word. If the drunk next door got into my room, it wouldn't count for anything, and neither would the rest of what I'd learnt. It had never occurred to me to include battered wives in my research.

'But, even if I had, it wouldn't get me out of this,' I thought.

When morning broke in the sky, it came as an unbelievable relief. I'd hardly slept a wink but at least I'd survived. I went down to breakfast to find Melvin there before me, the sullen expression gone from his face, to be replaced by the hollow eyes of a hangover. I ate in silence while Melvin drank black coffee. After he'd drained the pot dry, he apologized for any bad behaviour that might have taken place in the night and promised to take me straight back to Rosslare if I would only trust him.

He wanted to pay for my room, but I insisted on paying for it myself, which cleaned me out of money. I couldn't wait to be back home, but when it came to getting into the hire car with him, it was almost more than I could do.

I stood hesitating on the edge of the road. Melvin said he could quite understand the way I felt. 'I'm really, *really* sorry,' he said, looking thoroughly abject. 'This is all my fault. I've been a fool. The way I've treated you is unforgivable. But let me put things right. Just give me one more chance.'

For some reason, I did. Probably because I realized

that I had no choice. I mean, I couldn't drive the car myself, I didn't have a penny left for public transport and the only other available transport, as far as I could see, came in the form of a minibus full of nuns, who were leaving the village in the opposite direction anyway.

So when Melvin promised to take the main road, buy a map and never deviate from it, and drive to Rosslare without stopping, I got in beside him.

To begin with things went well. I looked out for road signs to Rosslare, pointing them out to make sure that Melvin took them. And he did. He took them every time, and seemed confident that we'd be back in Wales by early afternoon. That sounded reasonable to me – but I wasn't reckoning on the extraordinary ability of some road signs to have different meanings to what they say.

I know this isn't just an Irish phenomenon – I've heard my dad complain about road signs in Wales being just the same. But it helps to have a map and, despite his promises, Melvin still hadn't stopped to buy one, which meant that even though he followed every sign carefully, we ended up on the sort of road that's obviously going nowhere. You know the sort – narrow, winding, full of potholes, with grass growing up the middle and surrounded by peat bog.

I started on at Melvin, blaming him because by now we'd spent hours driving around and were nowhere near Rosslare. He insisted there was nothing to worry about – not for a former Boy Scout from the 21st South London (Morden) Troop. But I found his talk of steering eastwards by the sun and hitting the Irish Sea eventually worrying, to put it mildly.

'Eastwards across *what*?' I said, looking at the bog around me.

In fact, I saw more peat bogs that day than I ever hope to see again. More hills, lochs, rivers, silver mines, ruined abbeys, castles, remote pubs and signposts pointing every way except home to Wales. And, most definitely, more of Melvin too!

By the time he'd finished tying me in knots with a little help from the Irish road system, I hoped I'd never have to tangle with him again. He didn't try to force himself on me, or anything like that, but it was impossible to believe that our getting lost, yet again, was anything other than part of some cunning master-plan. It couldn't be a coincidence, just as our getting lost yesterday couldn't have been a coincidence. Melvin was keeping me in Ireland against my will. There was definitely something weird about him. He was a psycho, I decided. A deranged, pimple-faced psycho freak – and how I was going to escape him, I'd no idea.

As the road wound on, I got quieter and more furious and Melvin got cheerier and brighter. If he'd genuinely got us lost, I'd have expected him to be upset about it, but I swear he was enjoying himself. He was in charge behind the wheel; there was nothing I could do about it and he liked it that way. He kept trying to engage me in conversation, dancing blithely from subject to subject, not seeming to care when I didn't reply.

He even started on at me about the Mrs Marridge Project, which I might have talked to him about in a moment of weakness, when I thought I was in love with him, but no way was I talking about it now. So I said I'd made the whole thing up. That shut him up. It felt like a betrayal, but I had no choice.

'What marriage project?' I said. 'You didn't actually believe me, did you? You didn't actually think that I'd come up with a thing like that, halfway through somebody's funeral? What sort of creep do you take me for?'

We drove in total silence after that, neither of us saying another word until I caught sight of a signpost announcing that the loch — which we'd left behind us hours before — lay five miles *ahead* over the next mountain!

That did it for me. I couldn't help but blow up. 'Stop the car!' I burst out. 'Stop it *now*! I want to walk. Or hitch a lift. Or crawl on hands and knees. Whichever way, I'll get there quicker. *Let me out!*'

Melvin flushed but refused to stop, insisting that

things weren't anything like as bad as they looked. Perhaps he *should* have bought a map, he said, but as long as he could still see the sun in the sky, Rosslare shouldn't be too difficult to find. He started driving the car faster, which meant I didn't dare try jumping out. We passed another sign, announcing that three more miles had mysteriously been added to the road down to the loch. But even that didn't seem to bother him.

He carried on along a dense, green tunnel of trees that wasn't wide enough for us to turn around in. What we would have done if a car had come the other way, I dread to think. On and on it wound, until the last trees fell behind us and we found ourselves on a mountain plateau with nothing around us but grass, wind and sheep. Hills rolled away into the distance. There was no sign of the loch, the village or any other human habitation. And nowhere I looked – to east, west, south or north – was there any sign of the Irish Sea.

The landscape couldn't have looked more desolate – and our situation couldn't have felt more bleak. *Or so I thought until we ran out of petrol!* The car slowed down, then glided to a halt. At first I thought it had broken down, but Melvin's expression soon put me straight. He sat staring at the red light on the dashboard as if he'd only just realized why it was on. It hadn't bothered me, but then I'm not a driver. I'd assumed it was just some meaningless light, of which there were plenty on the dashboards of cars – but Melvin should have known.

Not that he saw it that way. 'I blame the road,' he said. 'We haven't passed a petrol station for miles. And the needle on the fuel gauge, it should have warned us earlier. This is not our fault.'

'*Our* fault?' I said.

Melvin tried to smile at me. It was the stupidest, most pathetic smile I'd ever seen in my life, and it just about summed him up. Anybody else would have had a spare can of petrol in the boot. Anybody else would have got a map when they'd promised to. Anybody else would have pulled in at a petrol station hours ago to ask someone the way. I pointed all this out, in no uncertain terms.

'If you're so clever, why don't you do something about it?' Melvin said, flushing angrily.

'I never said that I was clever – *if I was, I wouldn't be here with you!*' I shouted, and leapt out of the car, slamming the door behind me. If I'd stayed, I would have hit him. I really would. I'd had it with Melvin. Completely had it. I started walking away from the car. Looking back, I can hardly believe I did that, but the open mountain didn't scare me, and neither did the fact that I didn't have a clue where I was going.

'Where d'you think you're off to?' Melvin cried out, rolling down the window.

'Where do you think?' I answered. 'To Rosslare. Anywhere. I don't know. Anything's better than staying here with you!'

After that, there was no going back. I half expected Melvin to come after me, but he must have known I'd kill him if he did and wisely decided to stay put. I walked alone and, at first, my own company had never felt so good. No cars or tractors came along, and soon I couldn't see the hire car any more or Melvin either, thank God. I couldn't see a single house or any other sign of human life, but I didn't mind. I didn't even mind when the road petered out and I found myself on a rough mountain track. I simply carried on regardless, thinking that anything was better than turning back.

But then the shadows started lengthening and the wind dropped. The grasses settled and the hills all around me, rolling off into a sea-less distance, began to darken. Hard as it was to believe, another day was nearly over. I had obviously been walking for hours but now, if I didn't do something quickly, I'd be stuck in Ireland for another night.

Darkness crept towards me, stealthy and unstoppable, like a stalker on the street. I blamed Melvin for my troubles, cursing him with every swearword I could think of. But I was to blame as well and I knew it.

Melvin had been right when he'd said *our* fault. That was why I'd got so mad at him – because I'd brought this on myself. I never should have got in the car with him, telling myself I had no choice. But then, I never should have agreed to come to Ireland with him in the first place. And I never, *ever*, should have agreed to marry him.

But, worse than bringing this on myself, *I'd brought it on my family as well.*

I tried to phone them on my mobile even though I knew I didn't have reception. They'd be beside themselves by now, and it was all my fault. Poor Mum and Dad – what had they done to deserve a daughter like me? As I walked along, I thought of all the things I'd given them to worry about. Some parents had drugs to contend with, and sex and arguments, tattoos and binge-drinking. But they'd had marriage to contend with – and it had proved the biggest worry of them all.

'I never realized what I was getting myself into,' I thought. 'Never realized that getting married could be so complicated. It all seemed so simple when I thought it up. But I've had it with the whole thing, I really have. After this, I'll ditch the Mrs Marridge Project and never think about marriage again. I'll be a better daughter and come up with a sensible career. I'll make Mum and Dad proud of me. Make something of my life and pay them back for all they've been through.'

The only thing that mattered now was getting home. I prayed about it as I walked along, telling myself that the whole of life was a pilgrimage – this walk as much as anything – and God could hear me here as much as anywhere. 'If you get me out of this,' I bargained wildly, giving it all I'd got, 'I'll never look at another boy, let alone think about marrying. In fact, if you get me home, I'll show my gratitude by *becoming a nun*!'

I knew nothing about nuns, apart from the fact that a whole gang of them was running around Ireland in a minibus. But, as I walked along, I imagined converting to the Roman Catholic faith, taking Holy Orders and never fancying anybody for the rest of my life. I realized that this mightn't be some people's idea of 'a sensible career'. But I reckoned that once Mum and Dad had got over the shock, I could still make them proud of me.

I certainly had plenty of time to think about how I might pull this off. The track wound on and on, never getting anywhere that looked remotely like civilization. My legs ached, my feet felt sore and my stomach niggled like it used to do when I'd thought that I was suffering from cancer of the small intestine. The fact that I might be hungry, or that stress might be a factor, never crossed my mind. Instead, I cursed my weakness like a soldier whose old war wound had flared up.

My head started aching too and I even started seeing lights in front of my eyes. They moved towards me slowly and I couldn't blink them away. I imagined myself in a terminal condition, collapsing here on the mountain and never seeing home again. The wolves would eat my body and nobody would ever know that all those asterisks in my diary had been correct and I'd been dying all along.

That there were no wolves in Ireland made no difference to how I felt. I stumbled forwards, expecting death. The light grew and then I heard a voice. In my heightened emotional state, my first thought was that I'd reached the pearly gates of heaven. But my second thought was that this mightn't be death after all, but the answer to my prayer. Maybe I was experiencing an angelic visitation. Maybe God had heard me and was saving me. Maybe right here, right now, *my future as a nun was being secured!*

I started crying. A shepherd before a sky full of heavenly hosts couldn't have experienced a more profound sense of terror and awe. I sank to my knees, but before a single 'Glory to God in the highest' could be uttered, a very human and ungodlike voice said, 'Who the bloody hell are you?'

21

Kathleen Keogh

My rescuer wasn't God, thank God, which meant I didn't end up in a convent full of nuns, writing my story in some lonely cell. Instead, a woman in a nylon dressing gown and fluffy slippers loomed into view against the backdrop of a pickup truck full of savage-looking dogs. What she was doing dressed like that, driving around the mountain in the dark, I never found out. Kathleen Keogh was her name, pronounced 'kee-o' to rhyme with keyhole without the 'h' and 'l'. I'll always remember her standing on the track in her slippers, her toes hanging out of them like brown slugs, her untidy mess of hair lit up like a halo by the truck's blazing headlamps.

'I'm lost,' I said, instead of answering her question.

'You're telling me!' she said. 'Get in.'

Feeling halfway between a kidnap victim and a sheep about to be returned to its pen, I allowed myself to be loaded into her truck. Without telling me where I was being taken, Kathleen Keogh drove at breakneck speed down indescribably bumpy mountain tracks until a grey house loomed into view.

She led me straight inside. I asked for a phone but the look she gave me suggested I was mad for even thinking she might have one. She did, however, have a bath, which she filled for me because I needed it, apparently. It was a nice old-fashioned bath with legs on claws, in a nice old-fashioned bathroom that, with beads and candles, scented soaps in pretty boxes and an old mirror framed with seashells, turned out to be Kathleen Keogh's only luxury.

When the water was too cold to stay soaking any more, I went into the kitchen to find her hard at work. It was nearly ten o'clock at night, but she was frying eggs and onions. She'd exchanged her dressing gown for a big, green apron and tied back her messy hair, revealing a pair of eyes as bright and dark as sapphires, burning in a flat red face criss-crossed with tiny lines, like a busy road map.

When she'd finished cooking, she installed me at the kitchen table with a plate of food in front of me and the dogs at my feet, scowling up at me as if their only hope of happiness was that I'd drop something. On the wall over the table hung a painting of Christ, his chest opened out to reveal a heart ringed with thorns. I tried hard not to look at it and fixed my eyes on a framed photograph instead, of a bearded man playing a banjo in a show band. His name was Johnny Keogh and he was Kathleen's husband in his spare time – her words, not mine!

While I ate, Kathleen told me all about her husband, who was a useless waste of space – just like Jane's Carl, I thought, only Johnny, it seemed, was ten times worse. Kathleen's was a voice that didn't have a button to turn down the volume; it never stopped, it just went on and on. Perhaps she was lonely, I don't know. Or perhaps she was just the sort of person who couldn't resist talking, no matter who to. Either way, she finally noticed that I was dropping off to sleep and said it was too late to go out again tonight, but that she'd find me a bed and take me home tomorrow.

How she'd feel tomorrow, when she found out home was Wales, I'd no idea. But that was another day's problem – one that I'd sort out when I got to it. Utterly exhausted, I allowed myself to be led through the house, lit by a candle because the electricity had suddenly gone down, thanks to a faulty generator that was always 'doing that', according to Kathleen.

It was a bare old house, worn and shabby. Even in the candlelight, I could see that. The walls were decorated in terrible, unsympathetic colours, which tried to brighten things up but only made them look more desperate. There were no carpets on the floors and the furniture was mostly old and broken-down, with springs sticking out of chairs and scuffed varnish.

This was a different Ireland altogether to the one down on the loch, with its pretty holiday cottages and well-kept local inn. An Ireland off the beaten track, where houses quietly crumbled into the landscape, beaten by the elements. Back in the world I came from, people thought Jenna's family slummed it because they lived up a track, but their house was nothing like as remote or weather-beaten as this one.

But, however much the wind whistled through the cracks, it still felt like a home. Upstairs, I found beds full of children, and heard them sighing and sleeping, murmuring and dreaming. The wind might be working away outside, but they were safe in their beds.

Kathleen Keogh found me a place to sleep and I felt safe as well. She blew out the candle and I heard the squeaking of springs as she climbed into her own bed across the room, moving children to make room for herself.

I was surprised at how easily I fell asleep. But it didn't last long. No sooner had I dropped off, or so it seemed to me, than lights flashed at the windows and engines roared in the yard outside. Car doors banged and there was a din in the kitchen immediately beneath us.

It woke us all, and the children started whimpering. I was sure the house was being burgled – although it was hard to imagine what for. Kathleen, however, knowing better than that, climbed out of bed, cursing her 'bloody man, who's never there when you need the bugger, but always turns up when you don't'.

The children settled down again and fell back to sleep. But, for all her grumbling, Kathleen went downstairs to welcome Johnny Keogh and friends home from a night on the town – wherever that might be, in this godforsaken part of the world. I followed out of curiosity, peering over the banister in order to see what this waste of space was like in the flesh. Nobody noticed me, and I stayed there for ages.

He was quite a sight, that Johnny Keogh. Easily over six foot, black-eyed like a gypsy and as black-haired as his photograph, though with a thinning patch on top. His arms were massive and covered with tattoos. You could smell the drink on him, even from upstairs, and he and his friends were very hungry, which meant that Kathleen had to start on another round of eggs and onions – something she did as if it was a perfectly normal occurrence at two o'clock in the morning.

Guinnesses were cracked open and a record player was dug out of a corner. It went, as well! The electric generator obviously didn't dare play up when Johnny Keogh came home. Someone got out a banjo and someone else got out a set of pipes that worked by being pumped with air from a bellows-like bag, to which it responded by wailing like a banshee. Later on, people started dancing, and the last thing I remember, before tiredness overwhelmed me and I crept back to bed, was the sight of Kathleen dancing in Johnny's arms to the strains of Tom Jones's 'Green, Green Grass of Home'.

Next morning, there was no sign of him. Or of Kathleen either, for that matter – her bed was empty. But I did find a row of little faces looking at me, half of them with eyes as bright as sapphires and half with eyes as black as night. Kathleen and Johnny's children weren't too shy to climb on top of me, but they were too shy to talk when I spoke to them, and grinned and giggled and ran off instead.

I followed them downstairs, and found a couple of older children getting the younger ones ready for school, making them a breakfast of Rice Krispies and strong, hot tea. Kathleen was nowhere to be seen. The children informed me that she was out the back, working on the generator, which had 'done it' again.

After I'd had a cup of tea to wake myself up, I went to see if I could help, partly to say thank you for my bed, and partly because I'd done electricity at school and had found it an interesting enough subject to think I might be able to help.

'The back' turned out to be a bare patch of soil, scratched clean by hens to form a perfect dust bowl for sparrows. Along one side ran the walls of the cowshed and along the opposite side ran a lean-to hut that housed the electricity generator.

It was here that I found Kathleen cursing and swearing, up to her elbows in black oil. It was a windy day and the door kept banging open despite her best efforts to wedge it shut. I asked what was the matter and she said it was old age – the generator's not hers; it should have been replaced years ago, but they hadn't been able to afford it.

The shed door banged yet again and, remembering my Physics lessons on alternative technology, I suggested that the answer to Kathleen's problem lay in wind-generated power. Given the weather conditions up here, I said, if she junked the old generator and set up a windmill instead she'd never have to pay for electricity again.

Kathleen laughed at that. 'Tell that to Johnny!' she said. 'He loves his generator like a woman. Can't see the good in her, can't see the point in spending out on her, but can't see the point in letting her go either. She's fine, he says, as long as every now and then she gets a bit of TLC.'

She walked away, giving the generator a good kick, as if that was what she thought of TLC, slamming the door behind her for good measure. And it did the trick! The generator started moaning like a cow in pain, and children poured out of the house yelling that the lights were back on.

After that, Kathleen fed the hens, hung out a pile of washing, dressed the baby and waved the older children off on the school taxi service. Then, when they'd gone, she said she'd take me home. Her words jolted me back into real life. Hard as it may be to believe, I hadn't thought of home once since waking. It was almost as if I'd been caught up in some fairy circle and enchanted into staying.

But now the spell was broken. Kathleen dug Johnny out of the pantry, where he'd crawled away to sleep, thrust a baby at him along with a bottle of powdered milk, a pile of nappies and his instructions for the day. He looked as if he didn't know what had hit him.

'I'll see you later,' Kathleen said.

'When will you be back?' he said.

'Who knows?' Kathleen said cheerily. 'I could be away for days!'

Out in the truck, when I told her home was Wales, she didn't bat an eyelid. Nor did she when I asked for a lift to Rosslare. I could have come from just up the road for all the surprise she showed. She didn't ask me how I'd got this far from home, or anything else for that matter until we came across the hire car, abandoned and empty on the road where it had stopped.

'Yours, is it?' she said.

'A friend of mine's,' I said, wondering what had become of Melvin — if he'd headed back to the ferry or got lost in some local bog. Not that I cared either way.

'Ran out of petrol, did he?' Kathleen said.

'Something like that,' I said.

Kathleen smiled ruefully. 'I expect your parents will be pleased to get you back,' she said. 'First phone box that we come to, I'll stop for you to call home.'

She did too, lending me the money and listening in to make sure that I got through. I dialled our number, and it was Kate who answered, much to my surprise. I couldn't understand why she was there, instead of in school taking her A-level exams. She sounded as if she was crying and I couldn't get a word of sense out of her.

In the end, Kathleen took the phone from me and explained that I was on my way home, and she was to tell our parents not to worry. Oh, and to pull herself together too, because everything was going to be all right and you never got anywhere in life by sitting around crying.

After that, we drove straight — and I mean *straight*, no tangled roads for Kathleen Keogh, just one clear dual carriageway — back to Rosslare. I could scarcely believe that it was real after all this time and not a place of legend. We drove down to the ferry terminal, and the sea stretched away into the distance. I had made it at last! The Sea Cat sat in the dock and home was finally within reach.

On the quayside, we said goodbye. Kathleen lent me money for my journey and I promised to pay her back. She gave me her address and I gave her mine. She said she'd phone to check I got back all right and I promised to write.

'Don't worry if you don't,' she said. 'All I ask is that you don't regret a single thing you did – and learn from your mistakes.'

We kissed like friends, then Kathleen stood on the quayside waving me goodbye. There were things about her that I didn't understand and I guessed I never would. Things like why she put up with her life and why she didn't change it. And her useless, no-good husband – why she didn't change him too. Dancing round the room with him was all very well, but it didn't mend the generator or pay for all those Guinnesses!

I spent the journey home trying to work Kathleen out. I knew that Mum would never put up with a man like Johnny, but Kathleen didn't come across as anybody's idea of a helpless victim. She had too much life about her for that. If Mum had met her, she would have liked her and been impressed, and so would Dad.

But impressed by *what*? I couldn't say, and still hadn't worked it out when the coast of Wales came into view. My heart rose at the sight of it, and I forgot Kathleen immediately, along with everything else about my trip. Until now, I'd never realized how beautiful Wales was. Even my school looked beautiful, sitting on top of cliff.

By the time the Sea Cat had slipped into its berth, however, my feelings of excitement had turned to dread. I disembarked and walked along the seafront, past the place where Melvin had suggested we went to Ireland and I had said, 'Why not?'

It all felt like years ago, and I felt like a totally different person, rubbing my eyes like someone who'd woken from a long dream. I climbed the hill up to the town centre and caught the first bus home. The driver stared when I paid my fare, but didn't say a word. In fact, everybody on the bus stared, or so it seemed to me, as if they all knew I'd run off with a man.

I kept my head down all the way home, hoping that nobody would speak to me. By the time I walked up Goat Street, my stomach was churning enough to earn me triple asterisks. At our house, I braced myself to go in. The living room was empty, but, when I went through to the kitchen, everyone was there. And I mean *everyone*. Mum, Dad, Kate, Jane, Grandad, Carl and Imogen Louise. Even Jenna, Jody and Rebecca were there.

And the police.

Mum exploded at the sight of me. 'WHERE THE HELL HAVE *YOU* BEEN?!!' she said, throwing in the f-word for good measure, which I'd never heard her use before.

But Dad said all that mattered was that I was home.

Epilogue: Jumping In

The following week was best forgotten. Over and over again, I had to say where I'd been and try to explain why. This was difficult to do, even to myself. It was as if the whole thing had been a dream – not quite a nightmare, but only just. I couldn't believe that the strange person in it, acting so recklessly, had been me.

Everybody wanted to know who this person was that I'd met on the Internet, and how he had persuaded me to go away with him. I tried telling them that he wasn't the evil monster that they seemed to think, but just a boy who lacked maturity or judgement – in fact, somebody like me – but that didn't seem to be the story they were hearing.

Mum, Dad, Kate, Jane, Grandad, my teachers at school and even Carl – as if it was any business of his – all lectured me about the dangers of the Internet. Even Rebecca, Jody and Jenna had a go, and so did my GP, called in by the police to check that I was 'all right'. I felt ashamed for having inflicted so much pain and suffering on my family and friends, and a fool for knowing so little about Melvin. Apart from the fact that he said he lived in Morden and had once been a Boy Scout, I could tell the police scarcely anything.

It was hard to know which was worse, facing their investigation or going back to school. Here my classmates looked at me with curious eyes, as if my new-found notoriety made me worthy of attention. In some weird way, they actually seemed proud of me, as if what I'd done rubbed off on them and they were all suddenly coloured with glamour and excitement. Everybody in the school wanted to know what was going on, and my classmates were the only ones who knew — or, at least, they thought they did.

The place was rife with rumours, everybody whispering behind my back. I couldn't stand it. If it wasn't for Kathleen Keogh's advice to never regret anything, I don't know how I would have survived.

In the end, however, the fuss died down and an appearance of normality returned to my life. I spent the last few weeks of the school term sitting the exams that I had missed and trying to forget what I had done, while attempting, at the same time, to put things right with my family.

Kate, in particular, worried me. She was in a strange, calm state, as if a war had taken place and she was picking her way through its aftermath. She didn't seem to mind the way I'd sabotaged her A levels, announcing glassily that she could always take resits if she had to and apply again for university another year.

I tried to talk to her about it, but got nowhere. But then Kate hadn't been herself all year, and the pity was that I'd been so full of myself that I hadn't tried to find out why or done anything about it. I talked about this to Jane, who blamed the whole thing on Lucy Chan's death and suggested that what Kate needed was a course of crystal therapy.

'A shock like that is hard to get over,' she said. 'Hard for all of us. In our different ways, we've all been affected. I certainly have. I know I've had a baby too, but I'm a different person to the one I was last year, and we all are, you know.'

Perhaps Jane was right. Perhaps it wasn't only me who'd changed. Dad, I noticed, seemed to be watching less telly these days, and I even caught him talking about joining a gym. Then Mum brought home a brochure on Lifelong Learning and said she might enrol.

'Education's an ongoing process,' she said. 'Besides, I've been thinking. I've really got to stop punishing others for my missed opportunities.'

They weren't the only ones who were changing. Kate took up cycling, disappearing for days at a time with only Kendal Mint Cake for company and returning home with the wind in her hair. Even Baby Imogen got in on the act, discovering how to crawl, walk, talk, question things and flirt, all in quick succession. Jane took up speed-dating because, she said, she'd had enough of that loser Carl and a toy boy was what she needed. Dad said she must be crazy, because Carl was a good bloke. But Mum told her to go for it, starting a family argument that rumbles on to this day.

Grandad joined a church and signed up for every luncheon club and coach trip going. He hasn't married again yet, but it isn't for want of trying.

Rebecca threatened to drop out of school, saying there wasn't any point in getting GCSEs if you wanted to be a supermodel and her mum had a contact. Her mum filed for divorce, quit the bungalow, and had a go at modelling herself. In no time at all, she was living with the contact and was as thin as a rake. Rebecca was furious, but tried not to grumble because at least her mum was happy.

Jody passed her end-of-year exams with straight-A grades – something that nobody expected, least of all her, but she'd been quietly working and we all reckoned that she deserved it.

Jenna got mostly As as well, but no surprises there. She spent the rest of the summer dreaming of becoming a hydro-geologist, her ambitions still on course. Some people know from the age of whenever what they're going to be and they simply go for it, while the rest of us tread water. Sickening, isn't it?

On the last day of term, Ms Lloyd-Roberts got me into her office to assure me that life skills were the key to happiness every bit as much as good grades and I wasn't to worry about my poor exam results because, while breath remained in her body, she would see to it that I went out from her school fully equipped for life. The experiences I'd been through would prove to be very educational and I could always catch up next year.

'You have absolutely nothing to worry about. You can still be an astronaut,' she said.

I tried to keep a straight face. Now obviously wasn't the moment to tell her about my new idea to get an apprenticeship and train as an electrician. This was something that had first occurred to me in Ireland, out in the generator shed, but with so much else going on I'd forgotten all about it. Now, however, sitting beneath Ms Lloyd-Roberts's watchful eye, it came back to me with yet another sense of epiphany.

I went home that afternoon and started mugging up on everything I could find on the subject of electricity, especially the wind and water-generated kind. Mum and Dad were surprised by what they took to be my sudden interest in the GCSE Physics curriculum. But GCSEs were the last thing on my mind. I imagined myself in a little van with 'LadyNile.co.uk – West

Wales's F-email Eco-Electrician' written on the side. Mum and Dad would despair of my ever being like other people's daughters, and Ms Lloyd-Roberts would bemoan my wasted academic capabilities. But everybody has the right to choose what they want out of life, and if I chose to become an electrician – or anything else, for that matter: doctor, astronaut or even a wife – that was up to me.

I was really on my high horse. In one of Dad's *Guardian* supplements I'd found an article on third-wave feminism and the right to knit. It said that women didn't always have to reach the top and people who looked down on things like knitting were missing the point. That certainly made sense to me. I'd never had the slightest interest in knitting, but I promised myself there and then that if I ever changed my mind, nothing would get in the way.

'We can't all want the same things,' I thought. 'How boring would that be? Some people strive to be successful, and some to be rich or famous or powerful. But some people aren't interested in things like that – and who's to say their choices are better or worse than anybody else's?'

Some time after that, I went down the estuary to retrieve my marriage project. It took all the courage that I could muster but was something I knew I had to do. I might have gone off marriage big-time, but my project had still been an important milestone in my life. So much work had gone into it. So much care. I couldn't let all that effort go to waste. Besides, I didn't want anybody else finding it.

There was no fear of that, however. When I got down to the house, I found the entire plot turned into a building site. Diggers were in, bramble bushes were up, the house was flattened – and the Mrs Marridge Project had gone. I stood looking at the hole in the ground where it had been, hidden under a staircase that was no more, in a room that was no more, in a house that no longer existed.

'I don't care,' I told myself. 'I really don't. That's fine by me.'

But I was deluding myself. I cared really, and it came as an enormous relief to find pages of my coursework essays caught up in the bushes at the very back of the plot. They were torn and pretty unreadable, but I cleaned them up like buried treasure and took them home. I knew I'd probably never want to read them, but at least I had something to remember the whole thing by.

Then, later that same week, I had the chance of going out with a boy. His name was Seb Williams and he lived up the Fron. His sister went to one of Rebecca's classes – dancing, drama . . . I can't remember which – and she said he really liked me but didn't have the courage to ask me out. I thought about this quite a bit, because I liked him too, but, to be honest, I didn't have the courage either – not after my previous experiences.

The timing was all wrong, I told myself. And perhaps it was, but that didn't stop me thinking about him and wishing things could have been different.

I still had a good summer, though. Suddenly the holidays were upon me and I found myself spending long days lounging on the beach, sunbathing and swimming and teaching Lizzie tricks. Sometimes I went cycling with Kate. Sometimes I spent my time at Jody's place, helping look after her brother and sister, or went riding on Carningli Common with Jenna. Sometimes, too, I got trapped by Mum into helping cut the grass, or doing stuff around the house. She'd say things like, 'What happened to your interest in cooking?' to which I'd reply, 'What interest was that?'

At the beginning of the holidays, I wrote to Kathleen Keogh, telling her I was fine and sending her the money that I owed her. She wrote back, saying she was fine as well, and hoped I was having a good time. After that, I told myself I'd done it all – dotted the last 'i' and crossed the last 't', and could get on with my life and put my marriage project behind me.

But it wasn't as simple as that. All the way through the summer, something niggled away at me. It simply wouldn't leave me alone. Sometimes I'd manage to forget it for days at a time, but then it would come back. I'd be doing things with my friends, going through the motions of my old life, and suddenly this overwhelming sadness would come over me. I'd feel as if I'd been through everything and yet failed to learn from it. I'd list all the ways in which I reckoned that I'd changed, but it made no difference. Something was missing in my life, but I couldn't work out what.

One day, however, the penny dropped. It was too cold for the beach and I was in the swimming pool instead. A boy was stuck on the high diving board, too scared to jump but too ashamed to turn around and walk away. It made for riveting viewing. The boy's mother, desperately treading water, shouted words of encouragement to him. 'Dale,' she shouted, 'I'm here for you. I've got you. You can do it – one, two, three …'

But the truth was that she could have counted to a hundred and still Dale wouldn't have jumped. If his heels had been super-glued to the board it couldn't have been more difficult. You'd have thought that gravity would have forced him over the edge, but for three-quarters of an hour he bent his knees, ready to go, then straightened up again; held his breath, but then stepped back; tried again and again, but couldn't physically get his body off the board.

In the end, the entire swimming pool had stopped what it was doing to watch Dale's plight. His mother was almost expiring from all that treading water. The only person still swimming was his dad, face down in the water, trying to pretend that it wasn't his son who was causing all this fuss.

Then, finally, Dale jumped. Don't ask me how he did it, but the swimming pool erupted. Everybody, from the ticket lady to the lifeguard to the smallest child in the teaching pool, was on their feet and cheering as if Dale was their son, brother or best friend. As he swam down the pool, everybody slapped him on the back and said, 'Well done.'

Scratch the surface of life and you'll always find love. Sometimes you can't see it, but it's always there. In his moment of torment, Dale was loved, not only for what he did but for what he showed the rest of us, who could see ourselves up there, plucking up the courage to have a go, standing on the brink, not knowing if we dared.

When Dale jumped, we all jumped. And when we cheered, it was because he showed us that we could do it too. Before we'd entered that pool, we'd been strangers to each other, but just for a moment we'd been drawn together by an act of jumping that said life's for living – you've got to go for it, you've got to take the risk, you've got to love it. *What else is there to do?*

I went straight home after that and phoned Seb Williams. If I had the courage to run away to Ireland